TAKE ME

By

Allison Forbes

DEDICATION

To my mum. The greatest love of all.

CONTENTS

ACKNOWLEDGMENTS

First, thank you God for my blessings. I honour you.

Mary, May and Sandra, as the queen said so eloquently: You are my strength and stay. Thank you.

Dawn and Linda. Thanks for the jokes, you made it all easier. Thanks for having my back.

To my nieces and nephews. I love you and still need you, don't go too far.

To my sisters. Much love.

To my brother. Love you all the world, miss you even more. To all who helped me get back to myself last year, thank you. Your kindness is appreciated.

And finally, to Lenny. 100% love. Always.

Chapter 1

Waking up after a previous night's excess is never fun, and I'm not just talking about the godforsaken inevitable hangover, no, I'm talking about the gut-aching worthlessness that accompanies it when you come to the realisation that you've screwed up, and have once again let yourself down.

I peer over my shoulder and glance at the stranger I'm in bed with, and I just can't fucking remember. It's all a painful blur. The only thing I can hope for is that I had the good sense, and also the common decency, to have protected us both.

The figure besides me stirs and then opens her eyes. She looks wary, apprehensive, confused. Shit, I was hoping at least SHE had been lucid last night and might be able to throw some light on the shade that was yesterday, but she looks as lost and as clueless as I do. I close my eyes again and groan. This is the third time in as many days. I ought to get a certificate in fucking up, and a big round shiny gold medallion to accompany it. First place! the undeniable winner, I present to you Joseph Alexander Giovanni, the fuck up king extraordinaire. I swallow hard. God, sometimes I hate myself.

I force my eyes open again where I discover she is still looking at me, but now almost curiously, as if she's deciding if she likes me or not, if she had made a good choice in her drunken bed-partner.

I could tell her unreservedly she has not. I'm not the kind of man women should swoon or romanticize over. I look charming, act charming, I even have the patter down to a tee – but in reality I'm a contemptuous bastard. I hide the blackness under an illuminating smile, akin to someone who has multiple personalities. Funny Joe, good Joe, and then very bad Joe, and right now this Joe doesn't want Miss Curious here in bed with him. He needs her gone.

"Out."

She's doesn't move, save for rubbing her eyes and blinking up at me confusingly. Jesus, I think she's still half cut.

"I said OUT!"

Her head jerks back, and I know the message is starting to dissimulate.

'I'm done with you. I haven't the time or the inclination to make this a nice, pleasant experience. I need you gone.'

She swallows nervously and slides quickly out of the bed, she starts to put on her discarded clothes. No objections, nothing.

She is scared.

I've managed to scare her. She can see me clearly in the light of day.

She can see who I am.

*

"The bank's in trouble, Joe."

"I know that, I can dig it out." I stand rod straight, projecting confidence.

"You've had time to turn it around, it hasn't worked."

"I need more time," I reply bullishly.

Tim Robbins, one of the bank's major shareholders, shakes his head. "There is no more time – at least not for you. I'm sorry Joe, we're going to hold an emergency shareholder meeting, and I'm telling you upfront, I'm going for a no-confidence vote. I have too much money tied up in here for this to go belly up. You have to go."

I lift my chin as I feel my stomach simultaneously plummet. "Thanks for telling me face to face, Tim, I appreciate the honesty. However, we have ten other shareholders – you don't carry the decision."

He begins to stuff his mountain of paperwork into his briefcase, a sad sigh escapes him before he says gently, "It won't go your way, Joe, it's over."

I smile. "Why don't we just wait and see? Nothing is decided until the meeting on Thursday, so as far as I'm concerned it's business as usual." I smile a little wider although it's bloody painful to do so.

He looks at me with a mixture of incredulity and pity which make my hand momentarily tighten into fist. I hate people feeling sorry for me. I'd rather be hated than pitied. I stretch out my palm in relax mode again and stand there politely and just wait.

I can do that, wait it out. I can stand there until people feel uncomfortable, it's one of my strengths. Tim finally gets the hint and slowly walks towards the office door. I pray he doesn't look around because my stance is beginning to crumble. He halts at the threshold, his back still turned to me.

"I'm sorry."

I nod as if he can see me.

I wait a full two minutes after he leaves just in case he makes a bout turn, then collapse down in my seat, the strain of the last twenty minutes taking its heavy toll.

I've failed.

Again.

Unsurprisingly really, considering I spent the last banking quarter fishing in my favourite spot in Lake

Windermere rather than here at my desk.

But that's what I tend to do. Bury my head in the sand and pretend it's not happening.

I love a distraction.

Fishing, women – and my biggest failure? Smirnoff blue.

I open my desk drawer now, and take out my favourite brand of 50% proof and take a quick swig.

It's not nearly enough, but it helps to take the edge off.

I sit quietly for a few minutes contemplating, remapping, thinking of ways that this situation can be turned around. I'm talented, I can sell, people believe in me, I'm really charming … all that stuff – but there's something bigger than all that. Something momentous.

I don't care anymore.

I can't rally enough oomph to fight. The stench of defeat is out there for all to smell, and I am as the saying goes: easy pickings. At best I'm only stalling – days, mere hours really. It's futile, self-destructive. Stupid.

I pick up my favourite Parker pen handed down to me by my incredible father who has long been deceased, and reluctantly take the initiative.

I begin drafting my own resignation.

I would jump before being pushed.

*

"You did what?!" My friend Simon looked across at me in horror while I relayed the story.

"Resigned. I resigned. What else was I supposed to do? Wait until security arrived to escort me out?"

"Or instead you could have yanked your balls down from where they were holed up and stayed and fought."

I give a short bitter laugh.

Simon cocks his head. "What? Am I funny?" He gives a derisory snort. "The girl I am defending now in court has got more spunk than you, she didn't cut and run when things got rough at her workplace, she pushed back."

I bang the glass of whisky I was holding onto his coffee table. "The girl that you're secretly in love with, Simon, is being discriminated against because of her sex, not because she is fucking incompetent! Vivienne will get the justice she deserves and now I'm getting what I deserve. The two situations are incomparable!"

Simon first flushes at my assessment of his and his client's relationship, and then rallies back. "You don't deserve this, Joe!"

"Don't I?" I rage. "You know this, how?" I stand up and pace the floor. "You think I don't deserve this because I'm your friend? This is business, Simon! It holds no sentiments, you know that. You don't deliver, you're out, it's as simple as that."

Simon recoils from my sudden outburst because I'm not given to outpouring of emotions, negative ones at that. I'm positive, chipper, always up and ready for a joke. I'm the world's biggest comedian. But today everything is breaking down, and my ugly truth is revealing itself.

"Jesus Joe, what happened?"

I turned to face him, my face tormented. "I lost big time. I mismanaged my staff and allowed hunches and poor information to basically bring the bank to its knees. I couldn't stem the water quick enough, and the leaks turned into a full tidal wave and took me down alongside it. The least I can do is go with some dignity."

"And you're sure there's nothing more you can do?"

I shrugged. "It's done, they've accepted my resignation, it's over, I'm over." I walked over to the coffee table, picked up my glass of whisky again, and took a healthy slug.

Simon eyed me weary. "That's not going to help."

"It's the only thing that helps," I answer dryly.

Simon sighs. "What now?"

"Now?" I pursed my lips. "Now I take some time to figure out what's next. My banking career is over, I know that at least. Nobody's going to take me seriously with that shit storm on my resume." I sat back down. "I spent ten years of my life in that bank. Seven years of that working myself silly to get in this position. And you know the thing that really pisses me off? It took more than a few bad decisions to lose it all. I threw it away so carelessly. I should have stopped it, reined it in. But I just fucking didn't."

"Why the hell not?" Simon sounded almost angry.

I dropped my head in my hands. "I don't know. I haven't got an answer … can you believe that? It was self-sabotage!" I laugh bitterly. "I went on holiday, played golf, went fishing, basically just skived off. One of the junior bankers the other day contacted me, ran a proposal by me. Cory his name was – an incompetent prick at the best of times. His numbers didn't stack up, I knew it instantly, but I couldn't be arsed to go through it with him. I just told him to check the numbers again and then if he was happy, to go with it. I should have shut it down, or at least got someone else to supervise him, but I didn't, I just picked up my fishing rod and started stringing bait. As if it never happened. And that's only one story – believe me there are plenty others." I looked up at Simon again, my eyes somehow pleading for some sort of understanding.

All I got back was a look of bafflement.

We stayed silent for a few minutes.

"Have you enough money?"

I smiled wearily. "Yeah, I have money. They even offered me a nice tidy package today for walking away, but I didn't have the front to accept it."

"You should have taken the money!"

"I was stupid, irresponsible, and reckless! People are going to lose their jobs because of me. Some good, honest, hardworking people who don't deserve to. Yes, some bastards will go down with me as well, but what of those other people? The ones that dutifully turned up and did what they were supposed to do, they won't get a payoff – just their p45, a frozen pitiful pension, and a good luck speech written on some worthless headed paper. It doesn't seem right."

Simon roughly exhales. "Shit, that's hard."

"Yeah, it is, and yet I get the better deal. I've got a big house, fancy car, pots of money invested – although funnily enough not in my own bank. Obviously I had no real faith in myself." I laugh without any real humour, disgusted with myself.

"You're in shock, you need time. I can't imagine what I would do if I lost my job, hell it was much more than that, it's your career. You must be absolutely devastated."

I consider this for a moment or two. "And yet at the same time, strangely relieved. It's all over – I can sleep now, there's no uncertainty about the next day. It's all gone so I have nothing to lose now."

Simon looked at me strangely. "As I said, you're in shock. Maybe soon, when things seem more real, we can get together with the other boys and go out, relieve some stress."

"Yeah that would be nice," I murmur non-committedly.

"Don't pacify me, you little shit, I mean it. You need this, it will help blow off some cobwebs."

"Listen, you're busy, you all have partners, wives," I look meaningfully at him. "Love interests … things change. I'm a big boy, I can take care of myself."

"We'll always be boys. Gabriel, William, Jack … nothing's changed. We will always have each other's back. Know this."

I smile, perhaps genuinely for the first time today. "I know."

*

Right now I'm on my sixth large glass of vodka. Added to the two whiskeys I've already consumed, that makes eight large spirit measures and it's only four o'clock in the afternoon. Worse still, I'm not even slightly tipsy. I feel like I've barely touched the sides. I have a great constitution for holding my drink, unlike my mother, who is a pitiful non-functioning drunk. It's a blessed relief I am not like her, for she is embarrassing as she has no pride left, no dignity.

Or am I fooling myself? The apple doesn't usually fall that far from the tree. Maybe we're more alike than I'd care to admit? Probably I'm not as slick as I think I am, or hope?

It would certainly explain why at the age of thirty-two I'm currently unemployed lying on my sofa watching trash T.V.

Never would I have imagined I'd be watching

Ramona and Luanne from the *Real Housewives* franchise, cat fight and scheme … and worse still, preparing to set the record button for the next instalment the following day.

It's obvious, I'm lost. I tried to take a different route, I really did, but it appears I'm more like my mother than I'd care to accept.

Genetics is indeed a bitch.

That rogue DNA seemingly runs deep inside me and no matter how much I wish I was like my father, my inner reflection is all her.

I even look like her. And although I take my height from my father, 6'5", the dark hair and piercing green eyes, right down to the tiny diastema between my two front teeth, is all mum.

A raving beauty was a description people once used to described her. Not anymore. The ravages of alcoholism have all but destroyed her looks. Aged fifty, she now looks more like seventy – on a good day. And if I'm not careful I will be heading exactly the same way. I peer into the mirror on my wall and stretch my skin around my eyes and frown. I look tired, a bit worn-torn. My skin is taking on a slight reddish bloom and worse yet, at the age of thirty-two, I've been told I have an enlarged liver.

I need to stop.

Now.

I need some help.

Chapter 2

"Hello my name is Joe, and I am an alcoholic."

"Hello Joe!" they all chorus.

This is worse than in the movies. I smile, hoping I look encouraged. But I am not. I feel sorry for them. They all look like extras in some sado movie, pretending they are all so happy to see me, desperate to appear super welcoming when it's obvious that the bottom has dropped away from their own monotone existences.

I look around. Even the surroundings are dire. Grey peeling wallpaper, dingy yellow saccharine strip lighting above, light-blue carpet with a large red deep stain. Probably wine, I think to myself sneeringly.

"Joe, we're pleased you've come, this takes great

courage, Joe. Would you like to share why you're here, Joe?"

How many times are they going to say my name?

I clear my throat. They're obviously expecting an answer. The interrogation is apparently about to begin. Do I stand? sit? lean back nonchalantly, or forward expectantly? What do you do when you're about to spill your guts all over their faded blue stained carpet?

I sit forward. Polite is the way to go.

"I've been drinking for over seventeen years. More excessively in the last five. It's now gotten out of hand. I lost my job recently because I couldn't focus, I couldn't handle the pressure."

The crowd slant their head sympathetically, almost in unison. I feel the urge to laugh, but I pull myself together in time. "I was a banker," I continue. "Damn good at it – until suddenly I wasn't. I couldn't get up in the mornings." I do laugh then, because it sounds so silly. "I was a no-show at meetings, made bad business deals, didn't check guarantees. I was a liability, so they got rid. And I don't blame them." I shrug my shoulder because that's my story, in one sad little nutshell.

"Why do you think you turn to drink, Joe?"

It appears I'm taking questions.

"It provides me with the oblivion I seek," I answer truthfully to a lady in a neat plaid skirt who has a bad case of rosacea on both cheeks.

"Why do you need oblivion?" she probs deeper.

"Because my life is messed up. I come from a narcissistic mother whose only love above herself was a cheap bottle of cider, and a devoted father who worshipped his son and his wife and suffered immeasurably for it. Finally, it killed him, dealing with her problems. He fell asleep at the wheel of a car and ended up wrapped around a tree. He was thirty-four. It was a blessed relief really, he was the kindest, gentlest soul, but he didn't know when to quit. And while it was devastating, his death, it was also a relief, because he was now free from her. Imagine that? You're told your dad has passed away and the first thing you think is, he's finally at peace. How fucked up is that?"

Miss Plaid Skirt smiles sadly.

"Anyway," I continue, "I was then left alone with

her. Which meant ME clearing up the vomit, picking her up off the floor, cleaning her up. I had to bathe her, comb her hair, brush her teeth, everything. And no one came to help. She was lucid only when she had needed to be, fooling school, doctors, even the local priest. I was left to cope. And I was angry. Still am. Nobody saved me," I say bitterly to nobody in particular. "And now I am her. I'm a waste of space just like her."

"What's your mum's name?" someone mummers.

What the hell does that matter?

"Maria," I answered anyway.

"Nice name."

Jesus.

"So that's my story," I end abruptly. This is all too weird, even for me.

"Thank you for sharing, Joe!" they all chorus.

I can't help the smirk that unwittingly forms on my lips. These people are NUTS.

"Who's next to share?" Plaid Skirt offers out.

A thin woman raises her hand. She's dressed

nicely, expensively even, and even though it all the rage to be slim nowadays, there's no disguising that her slenderness is alcohol induced. It's leaves a different stain on you, does alcohol, you can just tell. You get a haunted look, not natural at all.

"Hi I'm Annalise and I am an alcoholic."

"Hello Annalise!" They all chorus. I roll my eyes, this is seriously annoying.

Annalise continues. "I've been drinking for three years and the authorities have just taken my kid."

My eyes snap back to her.

"I got so drunk one day, I forgot to pick my son up from school. It wasn't the first time either. Now he's in foster care and I'm here to get myself together and get him back home."

The group start clapping – but I don't. Because who puts a drink before their own kid? I don't feel sorry for her at all. I feel angry and I'm glad that the authorities took him away like they should have done me. I sit there staring, disgust I'm sure registering on every facet of my face, when I feel someone to my far left staring intensely at ME. I turn slightly and my breath catches in my throat when I look over.

It's a woman. A beautiful, exotic-looking woman. She's olive-skinned, with long wavy hair and light brown eyes, and she's not cowering or anything. She's staring boldly in my face. A challenging look almost.

I feel myself flush because I can tell she disapproves of the way I've been judging that woman, hell the whole group, and she's letting me know it in spades. After holding my attention for a few seconds, she blinks away.

Touché I concede, and turn back to focus on Annalise's story, now feeling thoroughly chastised, but indefinitely more respectful. It's been a long time since anyone has put me in my place and it's oddly refreshing.

Halfway through listening, I can't resist a quick glance back at her, but she's disappeared. I swing around to check the front door, but she selve like and has quite literally vanished into thin air. A gnawing sensation then registers in my stomach and I realise that it's disappointment and I don't know quite know how to rationalise that. I shake the sensation off, feeling utterly ridiculous, and focus on what's happening around me, forcing myself for the first time since I've walked in here to fully engage.

I endure and stay till the end of session, more out of the hope I will see that woman again rather than what I'm actually getting out of this, for I have concluded this isn't for me, this sharing. It's not my cup of tea at all. I want to tell the lot of them to stop snivelling, accept the blame, and stop bloody clapping every time someone says anything remotely inspirational, for it doesn't count until you do it. It's called pipe dreams, and saying is definitely not doing. Stop being so bloody sanctimonious and pull your finger out of your arse and get on with life.

You see, not all alcoholics live in denial.

Sometimes we realise we do need help. I know I drink too much and I accept no one makes me do it. The drink is simply a coping mechanism to a wider issue. And I'm quite aware I'm not going to magically conquer the world and climb every mountain when I do manage to quit drinking, I'm just hoping for a more normal life without the excess drama and confusion that comes along with it. I'm not going to get a position like my old job and similar second chances in those areas are all exhausted and used up. Simply put, I blew it. It's going to take time, if ever, to rebuild the trust that I disassembled because I let some people down badly. I know and accept this.

So all this heroic speaking, attention-hoarding, self-congratulatory bullshit that some people are spouting in the name of inspiration is rubbish, and worse, futile. It doesn't work like that. AT ALL. They are all in for a rude awakening.

I shrug on my overcoat, content with the knowledge that I'll never darken these doors again, and make my way to the exit. It's cold outside, and I turn up my collar against the cold bitter wind. I walk quickly down the road where I've parked the car. As I depress the alarm, and put one hand on the door handle to open it, I see her again. The woman at the meeting who gave me the death stare. I literally freeze in motion.

She walks up to me. She has on a long woollen

grey coat with an accompanying red scarf with sections of her hair ends tangled up in it like she had just hurriedly dragged it around her. She's walking quite purposefully towards me and looks pissed – and I don't mean by alcohol.

"Do you think you're better than them?" is her opener. I say nothing save stare at her. "Do you hold yourself in such high esteem that it exempts you from feeling?" She continues at a rush.

Mutely I shake my head. I'm shocked.

"Good!" she declares loudly and then flounces away.

"Hey!" I call out to her urgently, but she doesn't lessen her pace. Her temper is carrying along the pavement like the wind. She's practically a speedball on two legs. I immediately abandon my efforts to get in my car, and go after her. "Hey wait up!" I shout, jogging to catch up with her.

"What!" She stops and twirls abruptly. One hand is positioned on her waist, the other flailing in the air, and she looks combative.

"Um," I stumble. I'm not usually stuck for something to say but this girl has got me stumped. I start again. "I've obviously upset you. I don't know how …?"

I'm treated to a stare that could burn kryptonite.

"Okay, you think I was being dismissive to that woman."

"Annalise."

I wince. "Annalise. And I guess I was. But it's my first time at one of these meetings, and I was kinda uncomfortable."

"Uncomfortable? You were smirking throughout!"

I raise an eyebrow. "You're not shy in calling someone out, are you?"

"These meetings are not a joke, they're literally people's lifelines. You have no right to go in there and make a mockery out of it!"

That quickly sobered me. "I'm sorry."

She exhales heavily, wanting to spew more accusations at me I'm sure, but my quick acceptance of my behaviour has her on the back foot.

"Okay. Well … don't do it again," she says now with less authority and turns to walk away, and I reach out instinctively and hold her arm.

I don't know why I did it. Certainly there was no conscious thought behind doing so. She looks pointedly down at my hand and I remove it immediately. It seems I wasn't through being a dick today.

"I apologise for been trivial about the meetings," I say sincerely. "I also apologise for smirking throughout and now I apologise for putting my hand on you. It's not my attention to upset you, although I can see clearly that I've done so. Please will you allow me to buy you a drink – a soft one – to make up for the fact I got things so terribly wrong?"

"There's no need for that," she answers, a touch aggressively.

"No, but I want to. I want to make amends."

"Why?"

"Because I'm not enjoying seeing you so angry. I would never had been so openly sneering and judgemental about those people if I knew it would cause offence like this."

"Oh you would have just been more discreet?"

I nibble uncomfortably at my lip. "Probably," I admit truthfully. "I can't lie and say I'm comfortable or agree with all that went on in there, but I have no wish to devalue its worth to you."

"No, in my eyes you've only succeeded in devaluing yourself. What were you even doing here anyway if you're not serious about getting help?"

I recoil slightly, for her aim is razor sharp. "I am!" I defend. "It's just not my thing this group participation, spilling out your guts to all and sundry, I prefer a pill, some written instructions, and a review session once in a while."

She shakes her head animatedly. "It doesn't work like that. We all need help, and talking therapy is a big part in that, as well as sponsors, family, and routine. We just have to be big enough to accept it and not colour it with our own prejudices."

I don't necessary agree, but I nod agreeably. I can see I'm on a hiding to nowhere with this one.

"Are you always this plain speaking?" I ask with a smile in my voice.

"You learn to cut out the bullshit – you should try it some time."

I take a few seconds then, because it's solely needed. I definitely don't want to react off the cuff, and tell her to go stuff herself. Beautiful she may well be, but she could also do with taking a course in decorum herself instead of calling me out on my behaviour alone. But strangely she also intrigues me and it's a long time since anyone has. I find I want to keep her talking some more.

"Can we start again?" I plead, holding out my hand. "Hi, I'm Joe, I'm a raging alcoholic and sometimes, even whilst sober, I can make poor decisions."

Her lips twitch in spite of herself, and I can see her fighting to maintain the current status quo of indignation and outrage before she finally gives it up and visibly deflates. She gives a big sigh.

"Hi I'm Shakira, I'm in a terrible mood, and I've just taken it out on you, please forgive me." She reaches out and clasps my hand.

Chapter 3

Her hand is waif-like, graceful and delicate, but very, very cold. I want to rub it, get some circulation back, but I daren't. The owner of this hand is a little firecracker and I imagine, wouldn't take kindly at all to that liberty. Although little isn't really an accurate description of her, more like statuesque. She's in ballet-like shoes and she still manages to comes up to the upper part of my chest. And with me standing at 6'5 that's no mean feat.

She slender. I can tell even under that heavy woollen coat, but I can bet she's also athletically built. It's the way she carries herself. Like a proud energetic gazelle. Everything about her appearance I find pleasing, down to her straight white uniform teeth and beautiful bountiful lips that are slightly poutier on the top. However, her eyes are the showstopper, they are nothing short of magnificent. Very light brown, almost pale. And her cute nose with their tiny little freckles. Adorable.

Shakira gives an involuntary shiver and tugs the scarf she's wearing more securely around her.

"So that drink?" I enquire again. "I promise not to get handsy again."

"I hope not, more for your own sake," she retorts. "I have a black belt in karate!"

I don't know why, but that makes me smile. I like that she can take care of herself. I gesture to my car. "I'm just parked down there. I know a nice place a couple of miles away."

"I know a coffee shop just right around this corner," she quickly counters, pointing the other way. "It's only a two-minute walk."

I nod, understanding. That's street smart. She's just met me, why the hell would she want to get in a car with me?

I wave my hand. "Lead the way."

We walk quickly as we're eager to get out of this biting wind, and in less than no time we arrive at the coffee shop. It's a tiny place, more like a takeout as it only holds two small tables.

I pull a face.

"No judging!" she calljoes. "The coffee is great and it's empty so we also have a table. And heat!" She shrieks delightfully when a wave of heat from the overhead heater blows in her face.

Her enthusiasm is infectious and I dial down my arsey attitude and take a moment to enjoy the opportunity to spend some time with this vivacious woman. I pull out a white plastic chair and awkwardly lower my bulk into it. I'm stuck. Like really wedged. The chair has either been designed for a two-year-old or a nod to *Alice in Wonderland* before she drunk that 'shrink me' potion. I look and feel ridiculous. Shakira giggles when she looks over at me.

"Oops. Doesn't look at all comfortable!"

"You think?" I satirise.

"Okay big man," she helps pull me back up. "Take out it is. We can go sit in your car."

"You sure? I can manage here if you feel uncomfortable."

She laughs again. "No you can't, if you try and sit in that chair again you'll break it and they'll be down to half capacity. Bless you though for being chivalrous, but you know, I think I will go along with my instincts and trust you. The fact that you didn't argue about coming here in the first place indicates you're not up for murder tonight."

I bark out a laugh. "Funny girl."

We grab two coffees and hightail it back to my Audi.

"Heat, heat!" she demands as cold air fans out from her mouth and she shivers.

I dial the heater up to max, and reach into the backseat for a throw I keep there. She takes it gratefully and wraps it around herself snugly.

"Do you want to share?"

She looks worried for a second.

I laugh. "I'm cool, it doesn't take long for the heat

to kick in."

She nods then pops open her coffee cup lid and takes a joyful sip. "Best coffee in the world!" she declares.

I do the same somewhat more cautiously, as I am sceptical about a place that seemingly sells good coffee, but is kitted out with furniture more suitable for a kindergarten setting. But one taste, and I'm humming appreciatively. "Damn, it's good," I admit.

A dimple plays on her cheek and her eyes sparkle. "See? Just need to stop being so judgy."

"Judgy, is that an actual word?"

"Okay, arseholey." She grins to take the sting off.

"Still not a word," I mutter, but I'm enjoying her.

"So, shall we put it out there and discuss why we were in an AA meeting room?"

I shrug carelessly. I know she heard my story. "You know why I was there, I'm an alcoholic."

"Snap!" she says and takes another quick sip of her coffee.

I blink. I thought she was staff, or a supporter to

someone. I didn't actually think …

"Shocked?" she asks, cocking her head and looking at me steadily.

"Um, I—"

"Or disappointed?" she cuts in, her tone now sounding a tad defensive.

"Wow, who's being judgy now? I was actually going for surprised." I hold up my hand when she goes to interrupt. "And I'm allowed to be."

"Judgy not a word remember?" she teases lightly, but her tone is definitely more subdued.

I nod, and we sit in silence for a minute.

"Do you think I'd think any less of you? Why would I?" I say eventually. "I was surprised because you don't fit the conventional E- fit of a person who is—"

"A drunk," she butts in.

"Nooo, I was going to say dependant on alcohol," I correct.

"Same thing."

"But not how I wanted to say it." I consider her for a moment. "You know what? You know what I think? I think you're direct, spirited, brave, but self-afflicting like the majority of us that's struggling. I think you think you have to be a warrior all the time, but you don't, and certainly not with me. It's okay to be embarrassed or even ashamed. I get it."

"I know," she acknowledges quietly. "It's a defensive action. I'm working on it."

I nod and we sit there in silence again.

"What's the reason you drink, Shakira?" I'm surprised at the way that question popped out of my mouth like that. I am not given to asking people questions, especially being a private man myself. I sound like that woman in the plaid skirt. Nosy. Or at best curious. But it isn't as contrived as it might seem. I genuinely wanted to know as Shakira seems like a strong person, not weak and destructive like I am.

She closes her eyes briefly. "Because my husband died, and I was devastated." She now looks at me. "Still am. I'm also angry and hurt and feel incredibly cheated. We were supposed to spend the rest of our lives together, and he checked out early. He left me."

"My god did he commit suicide?" A thumping wave of horror drives its way through me.

"Someone shot him." Seeing my shocked expression she moderates her tone, maybe acknowledging that that came out much too flippantly. "It was a robbery," she explains farther. "We were at a gas station in America, touring Route 66, as you do." She gives a slight smile in remembrance. "I had got out to use the facilities, and David had just come back from paying for the gas. A man approached and demanded that he give him his wallet. David refused. REFUSED!" She shakes her head animatedly. "I came back to find him on the floor beside the car, bleeding out. The man had shot him twice in the chest. It was over very quickly, he didn't stand a chance. He had fifty dollars in that wallet. Thirty of that went on the gas. So he was killed for twenty dollars." Shakira scrunches up her face. "So Mr Banker, exactly how much is that in pounds?"

I silently shake my head. I know my answer doesn't matter; she's simply trying to buy more breathing space. "I'm so sorry."

"He left me for twenty dollars."

"No Shakira, someone took him from you for twenty dollars, there's a difference," I amend softly.

"But that man had a gun! He should have given the money to him. What about me? Did he not think about me?"

I exhale softly. "Nobody knows for sure what they would do in that situation, Shakira. I'd like to think I would have just handed the wallet over. But I don't know, not for sure. Anger, indignation gets in the way sometimes, you don't think clearly."

"I was so angry. With that man, with David. Everybody in fact. I just wanted things back to the way they were, I wanted ME back to the way I was. A happy, optimistic newly-wed woman whose only worry at that time was reading the goddamn map of the route we were taking the right way up." We both laugh at this point.

"I don't want to be this angry, bitter woman that has emerged," she whispers now.

"Hey, hey, it takes time," I encouraged. "The pain will lessen in time. I'm sure David loved you, he made a wrong decision in a stressful situation, don't hate him for that, forgive him, and it will hurt less."

"Look at you!" she mocks lightly. "The undercover therapist!"

I shrug. "It's just an observation, no patronising intended."

"You weren't. Deep down I know all of this, it just helps sometimes to have it reinforced. So thank you for that."

I take another sip of coffee. It's not often that someone is appreciative towards me and it feels a little awkward, a little hard to accept.

"Joe, do you have someone you care for, to help you stop drinking?"

I quickly swallow. Sometimes unsolicited advice promoted unsolicited questioning.

"No."

"Do you think it's possible to be happy again, that you can get a second chance and feel normal again, without the drink?"

I don't answer straight away because there isn't a simple answer.

"I think you find a new normal," I say carefully after a minute. "I think that someone like you deserves a happy ending and so will obtain it. Drink won't feature so much if there're is a focus or a distraction."

"You mean a partner?"

"A partner, a child, hell even a dog, anyone you care for."

"I loved David, but it's been three years now, I miss being in a relationship. I want another chance with someone else. Is that selfish?"

I snort. "Looking the way you do, I imagine you'll get a lot of chances. And no, that's not being selfish."

She grins. "A little typical of a man response," she gently rebukes.

"A truthful one though. You're gracious, open, good company, and not a trial to look at. I'm sure if you open yourself up to it, you can have it if you want. It won't be the same, you went through a horrific experience, and the drink has dented your armour, but it can be good all the same."

She looks curiously at me. "And what about you, do you get your happy ever after too?"

"You have to deserve one first," I answer dryly.

She adjusts her position in the chair, turning more fully towards me, her cheeks now illuminating a soft glow under the street lamp where we're parked. She shrugs off the rug as the interior of the car was now warm. "Why don't you deserve it, Joe?"

I smile. I'm aware it's not one of my charming ones. And I don't want it to be, because she's a nice girl and deserves more honesty.

"I'm bad, Shakira. Deep down. I have a darkness that nobody can touch. The least I can hope for is that I don't ruin anyone and take them down with me. And to make sure of that, I have to be alone."

Shakira looks alarmed, and she has every right to be, because beneath the exterior I know I'm no good. Beneath the surface, if you care to scratch it, it's rotten to the core. The outer surface is funny, charming, but that skin is not sustainable and is rotting at an alarming pace.

"I understand why today you were so pissed with me," I continue. "I made a mockery of where you found sanctuary, and I tend to do that. Anything good or even plain ordinary, I tend to sneer at or destroy. I don't want to be a bad person, I just am. It's hot wired in my DNA, there are people I care about, sure, but they don't really know me, the real me, they only know what I present to them. They'd be shocked if they delved deeper. I struggle you know, to keep up, to learn and remember my social cues, just to fit in, to appear … normal."

"I think you're doing just fine," she whispers.

I swirl my now cold coffee around in my cup. "Thanks for that."

"Do you want to talk, you know, about your mum, what you went through …?" she asks tentatively.

I give a small chuckle that is utterly mirthless. "No, not really, as I said, I'm not good at all this, it's not for me."

She nods her understanding. "Well … um thanks … you know for listening to me. It helped." We smile awkwardly at each other.

I'm destroying this now, she feels wary, she feels uneasy in my presence.

"Gosh look at the time!" she parries after a minute squirming.

"Yeah, I better be getting on, I have good tele to watch," I joke, giving her the out.

"It's been nice talking. I don't usually go off and sit in stranger's car sounding off. I'm glad I did with you though."

"So am I," I say sincerely.

She fingers the latch on the car door. "So, no more meetings …?"

I grimace. "I'll find another way."

She opens the car door. "I really hope you do, you deserve to." She climbs out and then crouches down at the window. I draw it down it with a touch of a button.

"I think you're gentle, warm, and kind and totally unaware of it." She touches my cheek with her knuckle for a second. "Promise me you'll get some help."

I swallow the lump in my throat. I don't feel pitied, I feel worried about. "I will, I promise."

"Bye, Joe."

I exhale regretfully. Sad to see her go, but aware I have no right to ask her to stay, even for a little while longer.

"Bye, Shakira, and good luck." I watch her wrap her coat more securely around her and then walk briskly down the road.

Chapter 4

I park the car in my double garage and access the house and whereby my kitchen directly through it. I look into the fridge, and a bottle of Pinot Grigio jumps right out at me. Damn! I missed that one when I was doing a clean sweep of my stash. I ignore it and reach for the pasta, cheese, and some meatballs instead. I gather my chopping board and start preparing the vegetables. It's dinner time so I have something to do. I'm chopping aimlessly, and then somewhat recklessly, my mind going back over the events earlier today.

I had definitely felt calm. I had enjoyed Shakira's company and my focus had shifted from berating my lot in life to something more positive. The encounter hasn't been a prelude to sex either, which was a new thing for me too. For a while I had felt normal, not forced, just content in my own skin. Admittedly, it got a bit dark in the end, but even that had been a revelation to me, revealing myself to a total stranger like that, I obviously had felt comfortable enough to do so.

But now I am back here alone, the darkness of my thoughts is starting to impregnate itself all over again, starting to bubble up to the surface and take me over. And I don't know how to stop it. It's like my skin is itching all over. My hand, the one holding the knife, is now chopping so fast that it's almost frenzied. I have to make a conscious effort to slow it down and then to stop. I close my eyes, take a deep breath, and will myself not to succumb to that temptation that I saw earlier in the fridge. But it's taunting me now, and I can hear the scream of its words. 'Come and get me, did you think you're strong enough to resist me? That you can make it without me? You can't, because you're pathetic and weak, and you'll always need a prop. Drink me because you're like her, and you can't get away from it and it's so unbearable that only I can give you the oblivion that you seek. Drink me, you coward.'

I swallow hard, perspiration gathering on my forehead, cursing myself aloud for the wretchedness of it all, before I finally give in and open the fridge and reach for that bottle, breaking the seal in one savage twist before taking a hearty slug. I chug it down so fast, some of the liquid drips down my chin and on to my pristine white shirt, but I keep going regardless, until I'm breathless, choking, what with the volume and the rate that I'm consuming it.

And then I pause.

I hunch over, gasping for breath, my eyes fire red, streaming with water, and my cheeks, chin, neck, and shirt dripping with wine.

I am disgusted, but not sedated. I want some more.

I want it all.

Chapter 5

"Joe, Joe. Can you hear us? Wake up, mate."

I frown. This is weird, that sounds like Jack. But how can that be my friend Jack when he's not in my house?

I open my eyes, and it burns like hell. There is a bright shard of light like heaven baring down on me. I immediately close them again. Dear God, have I died? Is that it? Have I died and instead of going down, I've been given a pass and gone upwards?

"Joe, you bastard, wake up NOW!"

Now that's Gabriel. I'm sure of it. What are Gabriel and Jack doing in heaven? I'm pretty sure Gabriel wouldn't be let up here, what with his potty mouth. Jack too, he's a sly irritating little fucker. I crack my eyes open again. And then I see them. All four of them. Jack, Gabriel, William, and Simon. My brothers in arms.

"Wha … what are you all doing here?" I ask in confusion.

"Do you know where you are?" William asks gently.

I look around me. This room is stark white, with tubes everywhere and heavy equipment. There's also an irritating noise that keeps on bleeping. I try to haul myself up, thoroughly disorientated. *Where the hell am I?*

"You're in hospital," says Simon, answering my unspoken question.

What? What am I doing here?

"Your cleaner found you, called an ambulance and then us," he uncannily answers me again.

I open my mouth then snap it shut again. I've just noticed something. They all look angry.

Which is weird.

I'm obviously missing something. The tension in this room is unmistakable.

"It's a good job she did too, because you bloody inhaled your own vomit!" Gabriel shouts in a sudden outburst.

I did?

"What happened?" William asks, seemingly the only one willing to take his time with me.

I reach up and rub my forehead in confusion. Because I'm not sure. The last thing I remember is cooking dinner. Did I choke or something? If so, why is this saline drip doing in my arm? And why have I got a stinking headache?

"I don't know," I answer truthfully. "I don't remember."

Gabriel tsks. "Of course you don't! How could you? Bloody hell Joe, we all like a drink or two, but I don't recall anyone of us ending up in resus!"

"Okay, take it easy," William butts in.

Gabriel paces away in frustration, in no mood to be pacified. "No!" he says, his voice still raised. "He bloody scared us, at one point, he stopped breathing, and they had to pump his friggin chest!"

I stare at him, horrified, my brain still scrambling to catch up with the revelations.

Are they talking about me? Can't be. I mean, I would know right? If that had happened to me? But as I look at them I see the distress, the barely contained rage, and not only do they look angry, they also look scared, anxious.

Immediately I want to say something, anything that will diffuse the situation. Maybe one of my funny quips that I'm famous for? I'm desperately searching when my stomach gives a painful lurch, and I lean over the bedside and ungraciously decorate the hospital's linoleum floor.

"There go my new Gucci shoes," Jack mutters, clearly unimpressed. He walks away to the far end of the room, covering his nose with his sleeve jacket.

Simon sighs wearily, giving me an assessing look before turning away also.

And that, right there, cuts me to the bone.

Out of all my friends, I'm probably closer to him. So it hurts like hell to see the disappointment in his eyes.

William, ever practical, presses the button for a nurse. She hurries in flustered, takes stock of what happened, rolls her eyes, and then quickly disappears to get a mop.

I'm embarrassed. I'm a bed blocking, stinking mess who's a nuisance to everyone.

Even myself.

*

"So this is your room. We don't allow WiFi, mobiles, or televisions, but you are allowed a letter a week from relatives or friends."

She smiles like that's perfectly acceptable.

I shuffle in the room and throw my holdall on the bed.

"Is that all you've got?" she enquires politely, her bright sunny manner grating on my already frayed nerves.

"I've left my Gucci suitcases in the car. I didn't want them to get stolen."

I'm pissed. I've paid top dollar for this rehab facility set in an imposing manor with beautiful gardens surrounding it and the inside of it resembles a prison cell. Not what I imagined.

"Can I expect running water?"

The nurse ignores the dig. "Lunch is at twelve, and then it's group therapy at twelve thirty."

"No," I say abruptly. "I don't do the group thing. I paid for one to one only."

"EVERYONE goes to group therapy in this program, Mr Giovanni," she says now firmly, aiming to squash my petulant stance. "That's is of course if you choose to remain here." She busies herself resetting the temperature in the room. "You will also get the opportunity to have a one to one with the therapists as well."

I grind my teeth. Forty grand for this shit.

"At two o'clock you can do some gym," she continues, looking pointedly looks at my little pouch. "Or you can play some snooker or table tennis with the other residents. Your choice."

"For Christ's sakes my stomach's not that big!" I suck myself in self-consciously.

"We leave you to some quiet time and then dinner is at eight." She carries on as if she didn't hear me.

I nod, but I don't give her the curtesy of eye contact.

"And then light out at nine," she finishes off.

"Is this a fucking kindergarten?"

No, it's rehab, Mr Giovanni," she almost growls.

She doesn't like me.

And I don't care a damn.

"Phone." She stretches out her palm.

She's enjoying this power trip, I think unreasonably. Slapping my phone into her hand, thinking right at this moment I want to tell her about that big blackhead on her face that's desperately in need of lancing, or the fact that I can also easily see the white roots coming through her sudo blonde hair. I want to tell her that she's not making this easy on me just because she used a jovial tone to begin with, or adopting a bitch one now to put me in my place. I want to tell her that I'm scared and I hate that feeling with a passion, and feel fenced in and utterly, utterly lost, and I'd rather chew off my tongue than admit this to her right now, but I could do with someone's arm around me squeezing tightly. But I don't.

Because I don't complain.

I just endure.

"It's for your own good," she says now, more gently. "All of this. It can make the difference."

I turn my back.

"I'm here if you need me," she says from behind me.

But I don't respond. I'm too angry. Much too angry.

Eight weeks later

"You have the tools now, Joe."

I nod stiffly.

"Just follow the steps and call your sponsor if you need help." She lays a hand on my shoulder. "You've got this."

I take a deep breath. "Thank you for everything, you've been wonderful."

Nurse Rachett, the name I categorised for her

when I first came here, has been my biggest support in these eight weeks of pure hell and degradation. She pushed me, challenged me – and also forgave me.

It wasn't easy.

Have you ever witnessed withdrawal?

Not pretty or dignified.

There are things that happens to you, your body, that you would never want anyone to see. Humiliating things. But I guess she's seen it all, and she had the good grace not to appear shocked or affected. She was the ultimate professional, and I'll never forget her.

"In the nicest way, I hope I don't see you again, Joe."

I give a wry smile. "I'm going to do my absolute best, I promise."

"Do better!" she advises mock sternly.

I walk forward and give her a hug.

She saved my life.

When I walk out the front door, Simon is leaning on his Jag, waiting for me.

I give him a chin lift and we both get in the car.

"I didn't know," he says to me quietly.

"I know," I reply in the same hushed tone.

"If I knew—"

"But you didn't," I interrupt. "Nobody did. Nobody is responsible for this but me. So don't feel bad. I don't need a babysitter Si, I just need my friend."

He starts the car. "Welcome back, buddy.'

Chapter 6

In rehab you have a lot of time. Reflective time they call it. You think about what got you here, and more importantly, what's it's going to take to get you out.

You also learn to think about other people, and how your addiction impacts on them. In essence, you learn how to say I'm sorry.

Writing was a good way to get things out that I couldn't, or wouldn't, say verbally.

I had a lot of things I needed to say, and had a lot of things to apologise for. I wrote to the guys, told them I let them down, scared them. I told them I acknowledged that, and that I took full responsibility. My former banking job got a look in as well. A lot of people lost their jobs or got demoted because of my destructive behaviour, somehow sorry didn't seem enough though.

I also wrote a series of notes to someone that most likely would never get to read them.

Shakira.

I didn't post them, of course – I didn't know where to anyway, but somehow it was important for me to kept writing them. I told her that I was embracing therapy. Group ones. I told her that I hoped she was happy and that I was determined now to be. I wrote that that I missed her conversation and her infectious giggle, and that I hoped she wasn't just an aberration.

Because I missed her.

Silly really, all of it. I didn't really know her, but somehow I felt connected to her. So it was important. To me.

I look at myself in the mirror.

I've undergone some pretty significant changes in these past eight weeks. For one, my skin is better, it looks far healthier. My hair has a shine to it, and my little beer gut? Gone. Got me a four pack right there - the remaining two can be worked at later. More importantly, though, was the change in my liver. I had managed to largely reverse the damage, and it was now functioning normally.

I had come a long way. But I had farther still to go.

The other issue I worked on whilst I was in rehab was my self-esteem.

As in I had a low one.

Nonexistent really. I felt everything was my fault. That I was unlovable, and not enough. I felt that I was useless, at everything.

I can't say those feelings have completely vanished, but I've taken great strides in overcoming the negativity I was so wrapped up in. Every day I stand in front of a mirror and tell that man in front of it that I love him. That he had been a small boy, and not responsible for what had happened. That my father had died in an accident, and I hadn't willed it, and that it was okay to feel guilty and sad sometimes and that I couldn't control everything.

Most days I achieved in doing that.

Sometimes though, I just stood in front of that mirror and just cried, letting it all out, or just letting it all go. Whatever, but I was definitely getting better.

So much so, a few weeks later I dared to go back to that AA session again.

I was hoping she was there. But she wasn't. The disappointment was crushing.

She had probably moved on, overcome her problem and now living the life she had dreamed. It would be wrong of me to feel anything but happy for her.

And I was, at least that's what I told my brain.

I wondered out to the street after the AA session and walked to the nearest shop, melancholy still alive and kicking me in my stomach. I needed some gum. Bizarrely sugary chewing gum kept the taste of alcohol at bay. I walked in and wondered down an aisle. I wasn't familiar with the outlay of the shop, and had no idea where they kept it. I had just figured out it was most probably up near the tills when I heard her voice.

"White wine please, yes, the dry one."

My footsteps stumbled.

Shakira!

And she was buying alcohol.

Before I knew it, I was right beside her.

"No."

She was startled, didn't expect to see me. I watched her visibly swallow.

"I ... I was ... I ..."

"Okay, it's okay." I soothed. I then shook my head at the shopkeeper who was watching, a little bemused, still holding the bottle in his hand he was just about to handover. "Just forget that," I told him, ushering her out of the shop.

"How dare you!" Shakira shouted, now recovered from her shock. "You had no right, now he thinks there's something wrong with me, he thinks ... he thinks ..."

"He thinks nothing. He knows nothing. But I do. Shakira, what were you about to do?"

"It's none of your business!"

"It is!" I counter furiously. "Because I care about you. You're two yards from the friggin AA meeting place and yet you were about to get sloshed!"

"No I wasn't! I was buying it for somebody, I wasn't going to drink it! Surely you don't think I was going to drink it?"

My silence tells her what she doesn't want to hear.

"Well fuck you!" she shouts crudely and goes to walk off.

I grab her hand. "Talk to me!" I insist, pulling her back. "You like talking, don't you? Well you look in my eye and tell me that that drink wasn't for you."

She stares at me challengingly for a few seconds before her lip quivers and then she drops her head.

"I only wanted a sip," she confesses.

"One sip could kill you, it nearly did me. I passed out and choked on my vomit."

She gasps.

"One isn't worth it, Shakira."

"You're making a drama out of this," she declares defensively.

I shake my head. "No I'm not. I'm telling you, Shakira, I've been through hell and back, but I've managed to come through it, and I'm all the better for it. You were right, I did need help, and you know what? I got it, and now I'm ready, I'm ready to talk now."

She shakes her head, indicating she wasn't.

"Come with me, Shakira," I plead with her. "Here me out. Please."

I see defiance still evident on her face, but I also sense some indecision, like she wants to be persuaded.

"What have you got to lose? At the very least humour me for a few minutes."

She sighs heavily and then follows me to my Audi. She's still angry with me, but she comes.

We get settled in the car, where she presumes the position of flight. I know that I have to get through to her, or she will just exit this car straight into an off licence again, so I throw off my inhibitions and start talking.

"I was neglected and emotionally and physically abused by my mother when I was a kid. My father did his best, but he wasn't strong enough to leave, so I was stuck.

My mother is an alcoholic. She's been that way for as long as I can remember. She ruled our household by her tyranny and both dad and I were afraid. She was five-feet-four, and we were afraid.

She was vile, cruel, and openly flaunted other men in front of dad. But he forgave her, because he loved her. I know that doesn't make any sense, but he did. And in spite of everything I loved her too because she was my mum. She was all I knew.

But I hated her as well. Sometimes overwhelmingly. It was very confusing.

When dad died in a car accident, I thought he was kind of lucky. Because he was out of it. I remember looking down at that coffin and wishing it was me in there."

Shakira covers her mouth in shock.

"I don't blame my dad for staying with her," I

stress. "He was a good man, and he tried to make life easier on me, certainly sheltered me from the beatings whilst he was alive. But after he was gone, it was open season, and I suffered badly. I was left solely in her care. I was twelve. I can't tell you the things ..." I bend my head. "No one checked in on me. No one. It was as if I was alone in the world."

"Could you not tell a teacher, relatives?" Shakira looks agonised.

"I did, once. A teacher. I was told that my mum had lost her husband and suffered enough and I wasn't to make it harder for her with my lies. That same day when I got home from school, I picked her up off of the floor and put her in the bath to sober up, my gut burned with the injustice. Mum was a chameleon; she could make people believe anything. I was absolutely helpless.

She told me I was worthless, pathetic, and nobody would believe me, that if I told I would go in a care home for liars, somewhere where they would hurt me worse. I was terrified. I got some respite when she was asleep, which thankfully was quite a lot, I could relax then. I began to build a structure for myself. A routine. I studied hard, determined I would make some money so I could escape. I knew it was my out.

When I was sixteen, I got a training position at a small bank, I was ecstatic. I left home as soon as I could afford a bedsit. It was tiny, damp, and bare, but it was mine and I felt safe.

But I also felt weak and pathetic, just as she had drummed it into me.

I was a big, tall man and still cowered to her. So I drunk to cover the pain, and developed a good coping mechanism, humour. I pretended I was happy, that everything was okay to take the reflection off of me. But inside … I was churning, the anxiety, the darkness that resided there …" I grimace. "I tried to offload all that. I slept with a lot of woman, I discovered I liked sex – and it sedated me, but afterwards I disliked been held, cuddled. I wanted them to go immediately. Which isn't very nice." I pause and look at her. "Still not. I try not to be ruthless, but at times I just need to be alone. I'm thirty-two years old and I have never had a girlfriend." I turn more fully in my seat and really look at her. "Don't you think that's strange?"

Shakira reaches out to touch me and I flay back. She's startles.

"I hate sympathy," I say, trying to explain my violent reaction. "And I'm not in need of any, I just want to explain. I don't mind people touching me, just not out of any misplaced sympathy. Please."

She nods, understanding.

I exhale, relieved that she doesn't take offence. "I drank, Shakira, to forget the scars that had become so deeply imbedded. Now I find I want to change. Rehab was the first step. It was bloody hard, but so worth it. I got back some of my dignity. I want now to help that little boy that's still in me, the one that's still scared and still punishing himself for being so unlovable, but I needed the man on the outside to first put down the drink so he can start thinking clearly. It's been eighty-three days and ..." I check my watch, "nine hours since I've done so."

A tear runs down Shakira's face. "I'm not feeling sorry for you," she says, quickly swiping at the tear. "I'm just in awe."

"I want the same for you. I want you to have more than what's in that bottle."

"I had a dream about David. About that night."

"I'm sorry."

"I wanted to take the edge off, I promise I wasn't going to get sloshed."

I nod. "I know that, but sometimes it doesn't work out that way."

"I'm sorry."

"For what?" I frown.

"For attacking, shouting. I didn't like getting caught."

"I know. It's okay, I get it. Can we go somewhere? Get a soft drink instead?"

"You sure you're not going to murder me?" She suddenly full out grins.

I set the car in motion. "I'll let you know on the way," I inform her with a wink.

Chapter 7

I take her home to my house. Of course I obtained her permission first. I live in a relatively modest house for a man of my means. Just a two-bedroom semi-detached in the heart of Chelsea. I have a large study, open living/dining room and a perfectly functional galley kitchen, and, considering where I'm located, a generous garden with a large fishpond which I just love.

"What would you prefer, coffee, water, or juice?" I ask, reaching into the fridge.

"Water would be good."

I grab her a bottle, and one for myself, and we both settle in the living room.

"You scared me a little last time, with all the talk of

darkness." Her eyes shimmer at me.

I feel a lump in my throat, and twist the cap on the water bottle, desperate to dislodge the impediment.

"I didn't mean to make you uncomfortable." I hate now that I made her feel that way.

"I realised what you were doing, just putting yourself down, trying to save me from you, when actually it's the place I find more assurance, more strength." She leans over, using her fingers to raise my chin.

"David's death, the repercussion of his actions, they still lick through me, but somehow you talk me down, you have the ability to calm me somehow, ground me, make me feel safe. For the first time since he died, I feel alive, like I have something to look forward to. Thank you for that, and thank you for what you did earlier at the shop today. I'm sorry for attacking you in the way 1 did, it was wrong."

"You're beautiful," I blurt out.

She releases her hold and laughs. "Is that a line, Joey?" she teases.

"No, I mean it."

And I did. I didn't just mean outwardly, which of course she was, I meant the way she walked, talked, laughed, her amazing eyes that expressed her emotions so vividly, the fire in her when she was angry, and the gentleness and vulnerability when she was calm. I like her.

A lot.

"I like you too, Joe."

I blinked as I realised that I had spoken that last bit out loud.

"How much?" I whisper daringly.

Shakira slowly leans, closing the gap between us and softly, tenderly, she kisses me. Before I can reciprocate, she pulls away.

"But we could never happen."

The immediate sting is a remembered one of rejection, and it takes everything in me not to react negatively.

"Why not?" I ask deceptively calmly.

Shakira takes a deep breath. "We're both addicts. It's not advisable that two people with dependant issues get together. You're doing really well at the moment, and you need to focus on your recovery. You shouldn't let anything, anyone, jeopardise that."

"We could just see where this goes and take it slow," I suggest. I can't believe how reasonable I sound when my stomach is churning. It feels as if something has just been snatched away that I didn't even get a chance to reach out for.

"It's not worth the risk."

"It's not worth the risk, or is it that I'm not worth the risk?" Against my good intentions, the negativity creeps in.

"I like you, Joe," she reiterates. "But you, we, could undo some hard work in the pursuit of something we don't even know will work out."

"We won't know unless we try. I want to try, Shakira." An element of fight flares within.

"No, I care about you too much. Much more than I initially thought. I can't take the responsibility of it not working, not for you – not for me either."

"Look I'm fine!" I burst out. "I'm in a good place

I'm …" I scrub my hand down my face and force myself to slow down. "I know that we have issues, but who's to say we can't face them together? We could encourage each other."

She shakes her head and walks over to the sofa where we had flung our coats when we first came in. "I have to go."

"Why? Because some psychologists somewhere deem we are not strong enough individuals, that's just the way it is?" I sound petulant, angry even, but, in reality, I know it's the disappointment and frustration of letting go of a dream that at first seemed so far away and then got so tantalising close. I try again. "We can be the exception, Shakira; you said it yourself, you feel safe with me, well you're my safe place too! In rehab, I wanted to get well for myself, but also so that I could show you the man that I could be. You kept me going. When I came out, the first thing on my mind was to come looking for you."

Shakira pauses in the act of buttoning her coat up, her chest heaving in emotion.

"Shakira," I continued, "I think we would be

amazing. Don't let others decide our future. If one of us feels pressured, the other agrees to step back. That's the deal. We don't let each other impede recovery. Bloody hell of course we can get it wrong," I throw my hand up in the air. "But gut feeling? I think we'd be fucking fantastic together."

She laughs out loud.

"At least give it a go," I plead. "Take a chance with me. I'm not saying throw in the kitchen sink, I'm asking you to dip your toes." I shrug and slap my hands at my sides. "It's your call."

I need to stop, I'm almost begging. But she's the only girl in a long time that I have ever felt this comfortable with without it being a predilection to sex, and somehow I can't let that pass, I'd be kicking myself a long time afterwards if I did.

"You ought to have been a lawyer, you make a compelling argument." Her tone has a smile in it, as if she's actually considering it.

I step closer to her and gently take hold of her hands. "I like you, Shakira. I just do." I shrug my shoulders.

Her fingers curl around mine. "If we do decide to see what this is, can we take it slow?" She looks at me through her eyelashes.

I heave a breath. "I think it's imperative that we *do* take it slow."

"And we stop if it impedes recovery?"

"I needed to get well, Shakira, for myself first and foremost. I'm no good to anyone else in the state I was. I would walk away, now, if I didn't think this could work."

"And what about earlier … what happened at the shop?"

"A blimp." I wave it away dismissively. "If you had had another focus you may not have even been tempted. You can get through this. Do it for me, I know I can do it for you. I did in part already."

Shakira eyes fill with tears. "I want to try."

I pull her to me and hug her. "We will. Together." I bury my face in her sweet-smelling hair. "I dared not hope you would like someone like me."

"You've been alone too long," she whispers.

"I've been alone all my life," I reply.

She pulls back, so we can see one another. "This feels right, doesn't it? I kept thinking of you, but I didn't think I would see you again, but I was waiting for you to come back all the same. Does that sound mad?"

I shake my head. "No."

She buries herself in my chest once again. "Tomorrow I'm going to go to a meeting, get myself back on track."

I squeeze her tight for a second. "We'll both go. And we will both support one another." As she nods, I feel my chest expand, and I let out an exhale of contentment I haven't felt in a long time.

After a minute we untangled ourselves and look at each for a few seconds before bursting out laughing.

"So what does this mean? Are we boyfriend and girlfriend now?" Jesus, I sound like a twelve-year-old.

'It appears we are," she says, smiling broadly.

"You know you're going to have to teach me, as I've said, I've never had a proper relationship before."

Her eyes glitter mischievously. "Don't worry, just do as I say, and everything will be golden."

"I don't think that's the way it works somehow!" I tease back, grinning like a Cheshire cat. I feel light all of a sudden, carefree. I haven't been this jovial for a long time. At least without pretending. It feels nice.

Scrap that – it feels bloody great.

Chapter 8

There are no blank, headachey, regret-filled moments when I wake up from my slumber the next day. This is because I know exactly what happened the night before. I put Shakira in a cab after we had some dinner and she's safe and sound back at her house.

This is a new phenomenon for me. I didn't sleep with the girl, and I didn't get wasted. I haven't woke up castrating myself, and I don't have the overwhelming feeling of guilt or the unenviable task of getting rid of my conquest in a civilised way.

Progress.

I sit up, stretch, and wait for it. I bound out of bed. I am ready to face the day ahead with a smile on my face. I pad downstairs to my kitchen and pull out the largest saucepan. I'm going to do a king fry up, I'm starving. I switch on the radio as I still like to keep abreast of business and current affairs, and the today programme on Radio Four filters out, giving me an update on the impending stock trade crash in China. I busy myself getting my ingredients together when my mobile rings out. It's Simon.

"Hey Simon. What's up?"

"Joe?" he sounds confused.

"Yeah Simon, how are you, mate?"

Simon chuckles. "Not as well as you apparently. You got some girl there?"

"Nope."

"Oh, okay, well, I rang to ask are you up for a boy's night out. We're not going to a club or nothing," he adds hurriedly. "We're thinking bowling or something."

I laugh. "Bowling? No, listen, I'm up for seeing you guys but I'm not going bowling, come on! We can go to a nice wine bar or something."

"No Joe, it's okay—"

"I'll have an orange juice." I insert. "There's no

need to change everything for me. It's makes it weird. I have to be able to cope, Simon. That's the only way I'm going to get better."

"You sure?"

"100 % percent. I have to be able to trust myself, and eventually you'll have to start trusting me too."

He exhales. "I know. I do, it's just ... we nearly lost you, Joe. We had no idea it was so fucking bad. What kind of friends are we? Especially me. I feel so awful."

"No, don't!" I say sternly. "As I said before, that's on me. It's not your responsibility. I made those choices and I could have asked for help at any point. But I didn't. In truth, all of us probably drink too much. It's become the norm. I can't now, not anymore, but there's no need for you lot to go cold turkey - just be more aware. That's all."

I sense him nod.

"What time, and where?" I ask.

"Stoad on the Rye. Seven-ish, if that's okay."

"I'll see you there." I ring off.

After stuffing my gut, I run upstairs, take a quick shower, and then hurry back downstairs to my phone, eager to send a Shakira a good morning text.

I grimace slightly when I see that she's sent me one already and try to quell the irritation that I feel at not sending her one earlier. I then take a minute to work on this so that it doesn't derail my mood. What does it matter who sent one first? I'm not less of a man because I wasn't fastest on the button. It's not as if she's going to leave you, for fucks sake!

I shake my head, and look in the mirror. "I still love you." I say to the reflection firmly.

I then smile at my madness. I wonder if she realises what she's agreed to take on? I go into my study and get on with the task that I've been delaying for far too long.

I start to look for a job.

*

By late afternoon, through banking contacts, I have secured four interviews the next week, and now feeling quite pleased with myself. It's about time I got back into the game. I may not be in need of money, but I'm definitely in need of the discipline and structure.

I check my phone again, unsure if I should text Shakira and enquire how her day has been. I missed my cue this morning, and I don't want her to think I'm not interested. But on the other hand, I don't want to come over as stalkerish.

Stop it! I command myself. You're doing it again. Obsessing. Go with your gut.

I call her up instead.

She answers quickly and slightly out of breath.

"What are you doing?" I ask, my mind awash with various scenarios.

"Ahh, I'm at work and I've just run up the stairs. I'm not as fit as I'd like to be."

I disagree with that statement, thinking of her long shapely legs and tiny waist.

"You look alright to me," I say, now suggestively.

"You're now obligated to say things like that, so I think I'll take that with a pinch of salt thanks!" she answers dryly.

"If you wish. By the way, I never asked, what do you do for a living?" It's just hit me. I don't really know anything about her.

"I'm a model."

Of course she is, her height, poise – she's fucking beautiful. Too beautiful to be wasting her time on me when she could have practically any man she wanted. I swallow the ugly.

"Lucky me!" I tease lightly. "Are you in a middle of a shoot?"

"Just finished," she says less breathlessly now. "What you up to?"

"Got myself some interviews lined up. I'm getting back in the saddle."

"Well done!" she praises. "Are you free tonight?"

I wince. "Sorry, promised the guys I would catch up with them, I haven't seen them since I've come out. Can we defer till tomorrow?" I bite my lip.

"Sure no problem," she answers easily. "Where are you taking me?"

"Out to dinner. We can have a question and

answering session. There's so much about you I want to know."

"Me too," she says, almost shyly.

"Shakira …?"

"Yes?" she whispers.

"I missed you today."

She giggles girlishly. "Me too."

"Do me a favour, bring your toothbrush tomorrow – don't worry, I'm not rushing anything. I just want to have a pyjama party."

"Are you serious?"

"Yeah. We're going to be up all night – talking."

She's silent for a few seconds. "Okay, you're on."

I end the call and do a mental high five in my head. She likes me. This beautiful sophisticated girl likes me! I do a silly tap dance on my way to my bedroom where I get ready to meet the boys.

*

"Joey boy!" Simon hails as I walk into the bar. This a little unnerving, it's the first time I've seen all of them together since my impromptu visit to urgent care. I steel myself and walk in confidently, styling it out.

"Hi!" I say casually to no one in particular.

Gabriel walks up and bumps my shoulder. "Hey Joe, how you doing, man?" He looks sheepish, and if you know Gabriel at all, that's very unusual, and not a look he wears particularly well.

I smile brightly. "Yeah, good, and you?"

He ducks his head. "Yeah … good."

I look to William now who gives a stiff little wave from where he's sitting, and Jack's talking to some woman and hasn't noticed my arrival as yet. "I'll just get a drink," I say motioning to the bar. "What can I get everyone?"

"No, nothing!" they say in panic unison.

This is almost funny.

Almost.

Jack spies me then and strolls up to me cheerfully. "Hey Joe, going up to the bar? Mine's a double whisky, cheers."

All the guys' heads shrivel to him like the exorcist.

Apparently he has broken the code.

"What?" he projects. "I didn't tell him to get one for himself, now, did I?

I laugh then. Because it's typical Jack, telling it like it is. No tiptoeing around for him. And I appreciated it, the honesty, for it breaks the ice and they all start laughing.

"Can we be normal now?" I plead. "I'm an alcoholic, not a child."

"Sorry," William says, wincing. "We were just a bit unsure when Simon said you agreed to meet here. We thought it might be difficult."

"It is," I say truthfully. "But it would be far worse to go bowling so …"

Gabriel chuckles. "Yeah I had a problem with that too. Have you seen the skanky shoes they expect us to put on? Talk about induce a verruca pandemic, no way."

"You're just concerned the shoes won't match your outfit," Simon scoffs. "Jesus Gabriel you should have been born a girl."

William laughs out loud.

"Oh and you can shut up," Gabriel whirls and turns on William. "Just look at you, you're a newly married man, and you've worn that shirt two days in a row now, a little effort goes a long way. You're punching well above your weight with Nicole already, so you need to be really careful."

William puffs up. "You say that one more time, Gabriel, and I'll …"

"Oh my god," Jack butts in, slapping his forehead in exasperation. "Are you two going to spend all night pulling each other's hair again? I swear this is just a prelude to some sort of kinky foreplay this back and forth nonsense. It's like communicating with a bunch of frustrated adolescents. I need some in intellectual stimulation, I need …"

"Who you calling a bunch of kids?"

I just stand back and listen and watch with a smile on my face.

Everything's back to normal.

"So, how's Nicole and the baby?" I ask William

who recently became a father for the first time.

He full out grins. "She's wonderful, and little Maxwell is great. I can't stop staring at him," he confines. "I can't believe I could be this happy and not burst."

I smile. William went through a lot of shit before he secured his future. He deserved a break.

"And the mother-in-law?"

He sighs. "Still not talking to me, never forgiven me for coming between Nicole and Peter. She dotes on Maxwell though so that's the important thing."

I agree.

"And you? How you getting on after rehab?"

"Yeah, I'm positive. I'm throwing everything at it. My life is slowing turning around." I pause. "I've met a girl that I like. It's very new," I caution. "But I have someone to do it for now as well." I leave out the fact that she's an addict too, as I know the guys will lecture me to death on this.

William sidles a little nearer. "And how's the other thing …?"

I feel my heartbeat spike. "I'm still giving her the checks."

He nods. "Look I know you've never expanded; I just hope you can work it out in a way that doesn't comprise your recovery."

I nod back stiffly. "I'll work it out."

I'm still closed, finding it hard to completely open up about my life. There are snippets my friends know, but not the whole story, and for now, I'm good with that.

Gabriel joins us.

"Sorry I was a pig at the hospital," he says bluntly.

"You were scared. I understand that."

"Got some good news that I want to share."

I perk up.

"Alicia's pregnant."

My eyes widen. "Didn't she just have …"

He tuts. "Gabriella is six months old! Don't be giving me no grief, I've had it from the rest of them. Plenty of people have children close together. It not a biggie.”

William rolls his eyes. “Alicia’s four months pregnant though. Maybe not that close, Gabriel?”

“You dirty dog!” I tease him, laughing.

Gabriel puffs out his chest. “Virile dirty dog,” he corrects proudly. “We’re both ecstatic.”

“Good on you, mate, I know how you dote on your girls.”

 He gives me a sappy look. “Yeah, they mean the world to me.”

Jack and Simon come and sit down and Jack pops his two fingers in his mouth and starts to make gagging noises, taking the mick.

“You’re going to be a lonely man, Jack, no one is going to put up with you. You’re way too hard,” Gabriel cautions.

“You mean opposed to completely whipped? You and William are both lost to the world. It’s left to me, Simon, and Joe to flag the standard now.”

Simon looks decidedly uncomfortable.

“I think you can count Simon and me out,” I say

laughingly. "Were beginning to see the benefits of being whipped. It gives a stirring in the stomach."

"Sounds like trapped wind," Jack answers shortly. "And believe me that's what indigestion tablets were made for. No thank you, I'll leave you lot with your hearts and flowers, I'll just concentrate on making the readies."

"It's no good, Jack. You won't be able to survive, come in from the dark into the light!"

"Never!" he shudders. "I'm a lone wolf, and that big prairie is out there for me to roam." He bears his teeth in jest.

We laugh. Jack is really out there. We spend the remainder of the night ribbing and teasing each other, and not one of us gets drunk tonight.

Chapter 9

The next day I wake up again feeling fantastic. I have a nice clear head and it's my first official date with Shakira.

I'm excited. I am thirty-two, and apart from a couple of times in secondary school, I'm going on my first real date.

I'm careful in what I choose to wear as I have always enjoyed looking nice.

Even while blottored, I always did it in a well-tailored suit. I was never a lowdown in a gutter type of drunk.

I wonder if Shakira is going through her wardrobe like me, or is she going casual? Fuck, I sound like a woman. Am I going overboard? Too late, I'm picking her up in exactly thirty-four minutes and it takes like twenty-eight minutes to drive there, according to the tracker.

I grab my keys and rush out the door.

When I arrive, my nerves settle, and I'm just really looking forward to seeing her. When she opens her front door, I step in and kiss her on her cheek, needing that contact immediately. It appears I've already become a needy bastard, and I need my Shakira fix to appease me. She doesn't seem to mind though, as turning her head at the last minute and catching me instead on my lips attests.

She looks absolutely stunning. She has on a red wrap dress which fits her like a second skin and her hair is down, flowing in soft curls halfway down her back.

I feel my chest swell with pride that she will be on my arm today.

"Ready?"

"I'll just grab my bag and shoes," she says and rejoins me a minute later now with her high wedged heels on. We're almost shoulder to shoulder and makes us a striking couple which garters some stares and nudges as we walk together to my parked car.

"By the way, you look beautiful."

She smiles shyly. "Thank you. It feels nice to dress up for something other than a shoot. You look spiffy also!"

"Your words!"

"It's an actual word!" she protests laughingly. "Anyway, where are you taking me?"

"My favourite restaurant. Sit back and prepared to be dazzled."

Twenty minutes later we pull up on Kensington high street. I manage to find a parking spot and we exit the car and walk hand in hand down the road. Once again, we illicit some stares, even some snaps by some admiring Japanese tourists as we stroll by.

I then lead Shakira into the restaurant, and she stops dead, shocked. And then she bursts out laughing.

"McDonald's!"

"It's my favourite. Especially the gherkin."

"You cheap sod!"

"Not at all," I defend. "Who doesn't love a burger?"

She takes a few moments to adjust and then steps forward with gusto. "Come on then, Mr Potato Head, mine's a super-sized, I skipped breakfast in honour of this."

"Don't worry, I'll buy you a McFlurry for afters."

We go up to the counter and order, and then grab a booth and sit down with our Big Mac meals and strawberry milkshakes.

"Well, this is certainly different!" she quips, carefully unwrapping her meal.

"I only take people I care about here," I say around taking a big bite out my burger. "Don't be so judgy."

She smirks and then does the same with hers. "Mmm, yummy, I don't like that cucumber thing though."

I stretch over and pluck it off her wrapper. "Best part, and it's actually a gherkin," I say, popping it in my mouth.

She pokes her tongue out at me and then takes a sip of her milkshake before delicately dabbing her mouth with the napkin.

"So, apart from frequenting burger joints what do you like doing?"

"You mean my interests?" I say, wiping my own mouth albeit less elegantly than she had just done. "I love fishing, wildlife you know, the great outdoors."

"You live in Chelsea. What's a country boy like you doing in the great city?"

"The city is the epicentre of the banking world, so it's really convenient as it only take fifteen minutes to get to work." It dawns on me that second that that's no longer applicable and I stop talking.

Shakira winces. "Sorry, but there's no reason to think that's over now that you've got yourself sorted."

I look intently at her. "I have different aspirations now."

"Oh?"

"I want to be happy, or at least content. I want to care about what I chose to do next."

Which is not really telling her anything. "How about you?" I ask her. "What motivates you?"

"To get better," she says bluntly. "To survive the lows without resorting to the immediate high."

I nod, understanding. She's so honest and open while I'm like a tangled coil.

I take another bite of my burger in order to pause and lighten up the conversation.

"I hate the term exotic, but that's the only way I can think to describe you, where do you, or your parents, originate from?"

"Ah, the exotic reference!" she laughs throatily. "My mother is Columbian, and my father is Jamaican."

"Beautiful."

"Yes, I had a blessed childhood. I lived in Jamaica for a while, and now that my parents have emigrated to the Cayman Islands, I go there frequently as well. It's a wonderful place to chill."

"They're still together?"

"Thirty years strong and still acting like lovesick teenagers."

"That's lovely. Do they know …"

"That I've been struggling?" Shakira sighs. "They know that I found David's death challenging. They're not aware to the extent. It would break their hearts. I'm not a fall down drunk," she explains. "I still get up, go to work, function … no one would know really. It's just that I binge drink, especially when I know I haven't a shoot. I then wake up and I realise I have limited memories of the night before. Not good."

"Have you any siblings you can confide in?" I ask that knowing it would have made all the difference to me, if I could have shared my load.

"Two sisters, older, and a oops younger brother. He is only ten."

I burst out laughing. "Wow! Your parents are hot stuff!"

She laughs also. "Yeah, I told you so. Anyway no one knows. I don't want to be a burden."

"You're not close to them?"

"I'm ashamed, Joe. They're all high achievers and I'm like some wino."

My eyes flare. "You are not! You're having a hard time, I'm sure if you explained they would be sympathetic."

"But it's shameful, Joe, I know you feel the same. It's like we belong to a club that nobody wants to join." She shrugs. "It's an uncomfortable topic."

I exhale. "Yeah, I know, and to be honest I'm the last person to lecture. I've felt like a failure all my life. That feeling doesn't just disappear, but now I believe it can be managed. I'm all about that now. It took much of my energy pretending I was okay and a positive person that when I stopped, I just crashed. I'm learning that I'm not superman and that it's okay sometimes not being the funniest man in the room."

She points at me and laughs. "You were the funniest person in the room?"

"Hey, I can be pretty funny!"

We laugh.

"It's hard though," she says, now slurping her milkshake.

"You've got too much ice in that. That's why it's

making that noise."

"Ha, that annoyed you," she says delightedly. "I'm learnt something about you! Slurping seriously annoys you!"

I roll my eyes. It's like we're kids. But it's nice. I'm used to bantering with the boys, but I'm not used to conversing like this with a woman. Usually, I just chat them up and than just bed them. I've never actually taken the chance to play.

"Do you really think we can kick this?" Suddenly she looks ready to cry.

I'm surprised at the abrupt change of mood and quickly cover her hand with mine.

"I know we will," I say confidently. And I meant it.

Shakira drabs at her eye with the rough paper napkin.

"Sorry, I've killed the mood," she apologises.

"No, you haven't, you're just having a moment. They're be loads more of those to come."

She crumbles up her food wrapping with vigour. "That was the best meal I've had for ages."

I take the cue. "Ready for afters?"

She takes a deep breath. "Can I have chocolate sprinkles on my McFlurry?"

I lean towards her. "You can have everything you want."

I get up to get the order, giving her time to get herself together, and when I return she's back to her normal self.

"Tell me about your job," I ask her. "What kind of modelling do you do?"

"Swimwear," she answers casually.

The nerve in my cheek ticks. I'm unprepared for the jealousy that at this moment balls in my stomach.

"Oh, that's nice."

She looks knowingly at me.

"What?"

"I don't usually get the word nice when I reveal what I do. I get 'Wow! you're a swimwear model!' or, 'Oh shit you're a swimwear model.' Which one is it?"

I grimace. "Maybe the oh shit? Not because there's

anything wrong with it, I've just gone a bit green around the gills about the attention you must receive. You're a beautiful woman."

"You're jealous," she says, sounding suspiciously pleased.

I say nothing.

"No need to be. I like you Jo Jo."

I swallow, take a moment.

"You like playing around with my name."

She raises her eyebrow. "Don't mind me, I'm only flirting."

"Haven't done that in a while," I admit.

"You miss it?"

"I miss the sex," I answer honestly.

"You never loved any of the girls?" she tilts her head.

"No. It was never the deal."

"You say that like it's a business transaction."

I consider it for a few seconds. "Perhaps it was. I buy an expensive dinner, go to a nice club, and then I would have sex. It worked."

"You never saw any of them again?" I look at her, trying to read her expression, thankfully it's one of curiosity and not one of condemnation.

"I have a few that I slept with that I would call up; I believe the term is fuck buddies. It was never any more than that, at least not for me."

She nods thoughtfully. "But you feel different with me? You didn't attempt to sleep with me last time. Maybe it's the other way around and you look on me more as a friend opposed to a potential lover?"

"Make no mistake, Shakira, I've thought of you and me in every position imaginable, but for the first time in my life I want more than the act. I want intimacy, and I want you to want that with me as well."

"I do," she whispers, sounding moved.

"I love spending time with you," I tell her frankly.

"Humph, I'm a cheap date you mean," she scoffs, breaking the intensity.

I laugh out loud. "Firstly, there's no need to impress you. I can tell you're a very accomplished, self-efficient woman, and secondly, by the way, this restaurant is world renowned."

"Yes, and the first one that I've been to that also hands out a toy."

"Yes, but it was very nice of him to give it to you since technically you didn't get the happy meal."

"Top guy!" she mumbles dryly.

I gather up our rubbish and place it in the nearest swing bin. "Ready to go?"

She stands reluctantly. "Well … this was nice—"

"Hey," I interrupt laughingly. "The date's not over, in fact it's just beginning. Did you bring your toothbrush like I asked you?"

She looks lost.

"I take that as a no, and I guess by the size of that bag, you haven't brought any sleepwear either?"

She giggles. "I thought you were kidding."

"We can stop in a chemist on the way to mine, and a shirt of mine will do to sleep in." I grab her hand. "You promised me a sleepover."

*

When we reached mine, I immediately set up the fire in my log burner as it was still cold outside and also fetched a throw from my bedroom.

I patted the sofa and beckoned her over.

"Sit with me?" I ask her.

She immediately moves to snuggle in beside me.

"This part of the date, we really get to know one another, alright?"

"Okay," she agrees happily, flicking her high wedges off and making herself more comfortable.

I draw the throw around us. "This cover protects us, we can say anything, and we're safe."

She smiles and grips my hand. "We're safe here," she echoes.

"My mum still frightens me," I say boldly. "When I see her, I still feel physically sick. I'm not scared of a lot of things, but I am of her. Still."

Shakira doesn't blink, her full attention is on me.

"I see myself in her, and that terrifies me," I continue. "She has mental health problems and I think that's how I'm going to end up too. No matter how I try to distance myself, it's something that bears heavily on me."

"It doesn't always follow. You could take after your dad," Shakira says softly.

I exhale roughly. "I know, but I can't help it. It's like a mental block. She is everything I don't want to be. I look like her, drink like her. Inside … inside I'm like her."

"No, that isn't true. You're a good man, Joe. She didn't love you enough, that's why you think that. She only loved you as much as she was able."

I scoff. "Which wasn't a whole lot. I don't remember her ever hugging me, holding my hand, nothing. There is one memory though. One day bizarrely we decided to bake dad a cake, it wasn't his birthday or anything, it was a spur of the moment thing. I was excited, it was the first real thing we were going to do together, we discovered, however, we were out of eggs, so mum went to the shop to buy some. She came back with wine. And that was that." I exhale. "Dad made up for it though. Okay, he wasn't overly affectionate, but I knew he loved me. We would go fishing. A lot. He took me out of the environment as much as possible. He would talk and tell me that she didn't mean it, she couldn't help it. He felt bad about the situation, but he loved her. Maybe he knew another side to her, and he was trying to get it back – I didn't know. But he didn't foresee him going before her, that's for sure. He wouldn't have left me alone to deal with it if he thought there was a viable possibility that she would outlive him. See, she was bad, even then." I shook my head sadly. "After he died, I felt so alone. She started on me in spades then. It wasn't just the beatings, it was the humiliation. One day she made me eat off the floor because I didn't wash up a plate properly. She said I didn't deserve dishes like normal people. She stood over me laughing the whole time.

By the time I was fourteen, I was six-foot-one and I had some bulk to me then as well. She was tiny. I could have fought back, but I knew if I put my hand on her I could kill her. So I didn't. The anger swirling inside was dangerous, but I contained it."

"You're not like her, I can tell you that absolutely."

Shakira looks deep into my eyes. "You feel deeply, you hurt much, and you're loving and kind, those are not traits of a narcissist. Those are traits of a man that wants to be loved and needed. You're able to reflect now, see how you can be better. You're a good man, Joe, I think you're amazing. You're not being the big man or pretending to be macho, you're able to be vulnerable."

"You think me weak?"

She shook her head vigorously. "No, I think you're incredibly strong to have survived that without lashing back. You have the ability to reach people." She points to her chest. "In here, really connect. You're very different to your mother, and in fact very different to my husband David."

"Why so different from David?" I ask curiously.

"David was the love of my life, Joe, but he was too cocky. He didn't care what people thought of him, he just bulldozed his way through. That of course has it's good points, but it also rubbed people up the wrong way too. There is no question he loved me, I know that, but he didn't have the ability to step down, to humble himself. He only saw things one way. There's no way he would have stood down to that gunman, I bet he said something insulting. I bet he didn't think of me at all in that moment."

"No one has a right to take someone's life because they're cocky," I insert.

"No, but I bet you would have thought about your family, rather than just winning. If you had a wife, Joe, and a possibility of a family, a future with someone you loved, at that moment, you would have begged for your life, you most certainly would not have goated him."

"I wouldn't have wanted anyone to take me from you."

Shakira closes her eyes, seemingly deeply affected. "Thank you. I needed to be told I was worth more."

I brush the hair off her forehead and stare right in her eyes. "You're worth more. You're worth so much more." I lean down and brush her lips with mine.

We kiss and it's like one entity finally coming together. All the Ying Yangs, all the stars, every piece of bullshit that you've ever scoffed at, happens. And I know immediately I've found an obsession.

Her.

Chapter 10

I'm good at making love, and particularly good at kissing. I've honed my skills quite indiscriminately and I remain confident in that aspect of my life. But this is like the first time and I'm … What's the saying?

I am woke.

Her lips taste like peaches. Literally. And I am a thirsty boy.

She breaks off with a little laugh and I realise I've nearly eaten her whole.

"Sorry, got a bit carried away," I say apologetically.

"That's okay," she says, looking a little flushed. "It's just that I'm a bit out of practice."

I hanker up slightly, giving her some space.

"I wanted to do that from the very first time I saw you, when you were giving me that death stare from inside that meeting room."

"Ha, and I wanted to obliterate *you* by pupil beam."

"Nearly did," I agree. "But I respected that you had the balls to do that in the first place. Also, the confrontation out on the street afterwards? Well, that was nothing sort of magnificent."

Shakira dissolves in a fit of giggles. "I was pretty fierce, wasn't I?"

"Just as well I admire strong women. But on a serious note, Shakira, you helped me. In rehab, when I had nothing else, I clung on to the idea of you, of us. I never imagined you would really want me, but I did hope." I give a self-conscious laugh. "I even wrote letters to you."

Shakira jerks up alert. "You did? I never got them!"

I give a wry smile. "I didn't post them. Didn't have an address to post them to. I just wanted to let you know how I was doing, and writing down what I wanted to say to you was therapeutic, like we were connecting or something."

"Can I read them?" she asks softly.

I swallow. "I don't think I'm ready," I laugh. "I don't think you're ready either."

She nods understanding.

We're silent for a few minutes. It doesn't feel uncomfortable, it feels like we are allowing each other to absorb. I like that, that I can do this with her. She's not self-conscious and asking what this means, she's just making space.

"I think I'm falling in love with you." My tone sounds casual, impersonal even.

Shakira doesn't overly react either, just offers a secretive smile.

I snuggle down in the sofa, get her comfortable, and wrap my arms around her, and we stay there until darkness falls and we go up to bed.

We sleep together. As in, in the same bed. But we don't have sex. Admittedly we got to third base, but we don't take that leap. This is special to us, and we don't want to mess it up. She's come to mean so much, and this is her first relationship after David, so it's a big deal.

I jump out of bed and go downstairs to make us some breakfast. Note to mind: Shakira is not an early riser. Admittedly, it's only seven o'clock, but it was like rising the dead.

In the end I decide to leave her in bed and go make us a big fry up to help tempt her down. As I'm getting everything together, I hear a knock on the door. I'm surprised as I don't get callers this early, departures yes, but not incomers.

I open the door and I see Jack on my doorstep grinning ear to ear.

I stand there staring at him until he pushes past and steps into my hallway.

"Shut the door, it's bloody freezing out there," he advises, now stepping into my kitchen. "This smells great, I was hoping you were up, I'm starving." He grabs the frying pan and shakes it firmly as the eggs are now beginning to stick to the bottom. I wander in the room like someone dazed and pluck the frying pan from him.

"What are you doing here?" I glance pointedly at the clock.

"Not early to a working man," he tells me smugly. "I'm starving. Mum and my sisters have descended on me and I don't have any peace in my house, so I've decided to have breakfast with you." He smiles broadly like he's doing me a favour.

At that moment I hear movement upstairs.

"Um, it's not a good time."

Jack waves me away. "One of your girls upstairs? Don't worry, I'm not shy, this isn't the first time I've stumbled on them." To my horror, he goes to the foot of the stairs and shouts up.

"Breakfast in ten, don't come down naked!"

He comes back into the kitchen, getting some bacon out of the fridge.

And where am I? What am I doing? Nothing, because I'm bloody rooted to the spot.

Now, my friend Jack. He's a good guy. He's fun, he's there for you if you need, but he's also the most annoying, tackless, mercurial, difficult, hard-headed man you could ever wish to come across.

In your whole life.

"Jack get the fuck out!"

"Oh don't go all moody, I thought you had stopped drinking?"

My eyes widen and I'm only one step from hauling him out when Shakira suddenly appears around the door. Thankfully she's put on some pyjama bottoms now and is decently covered.

"Morning!" he says to her in a singsong voice whilst busy frying the bacon. "Take a seat, this will be ready in no time. Joe, come on, get the toast ready!" He looks at me and then tuts as if he's long suffering trying to manage me.

Shakira, her mouth slightly ajar, slithers in and takes a seat at the table mouthing to me discreetly, 'Who??"

I shake my head quickly and get ready to tackle my oblivious friend.

"You're not staying."

He pulls a disapproving face. "You've been

drinking and have a hangover, don't you?" He put the spatula down. "Do you want me to call rehab, we can get you back in there before noon."

"I—"

"Don't worry," he interrupts. "Apparently it's quite common to have a relapse. I'm sure your little friend won't mind leaving so that we can make arrangements." He turns to Shakira. "Listen, Joe has a little problem, would you mind—"

"Jack! Get the fuck out of my house!"

Jack looks taken back. "After all I've done for you, I came to see you while you were in hospital, you ruined my Gucci shoes. I've come here today to cook you breakfast to make sure you're eating. You didn't really think I would be run out of my house by women, did you? No I came here stealthy under that guise to make sure you're okay. That's the kind of guy I am! Just because you're embarrassed in front of one of your groupies …"

I'm standing there open-mouthed when Shakira starts laughing. I mean belly laughs until she nearly drops off her chair.

Jack looks in astonishment at her. "Is she drunk?" he whispers.

Shakira laughs harder.

I first look at Jack standing there looking so confused, then at Shakira literally gulping for air, before slowly, inexplicably, I begin laughing also.

Jack looks stunned. He looks around him, sees nothing as the cause of our mirth, then after a few seconds he collapses laughing too.

After a few minutes we stop, tears streaming down our faces and it's then when he asks;

"What are we laughing at?"

Chapter 11

We put up with Jack's company for another half hour before I'm forced to put him out. Bodily.

Shakira has a shoot so she has to go home to get ready. I drive her there and offer to accompany her to work since I have nothing else to do. Luckily, I have interviews lined up tomorrow, so it won't be long before I'm feeling more useful.

Shakira emerges from her bedroom five minutes later, now dressed in a high-neck sweater and black mini skirt with thick black tights and high ankle booties. With her height and poise, she looks every inch a supermodel, which I am proud, but also very aware off.

When we get there to the shoot, we run the gauntlet of interested stares and nudges from people all the way up to the fifth floor of the building, and then she is besieged by the photographers and staff swarming her, giving her hugs and kisses like I wasn't even there.

I am partly appeased by the fact most of the men here are gay and are not interested in her in that way, but there are a couple of guys that I find I have to give hard looks to in order for them to think twice before getting too friendly. Shakira seems blissfully unaware, however, and that goes a long way to calming me.

Jealousy is not an emotion I've encountered in myself before, but I guess it demonstrates I'm not completely dead inside, and that my natural instinct are awaking because I'm feeling super protective right now and right on my game.

I find a chair out of the way and wait for Shakira who's currently in the changing room to come out for the first scene. I flick uninterestingly through one of the fashion magazines on the coffee table and occasionally check my mobile messages, but I'm like a bloody Meerkat watching over her, making sure that no one but the stylists goes near that changing room.

Then she walks out. And I nearly swallow my tongue.

She's in a scarlet barely-there bikini and high-heel plastic see-through mules. I feel my seat glands explode.

She walks by me and into the scene where she poses on a sun lounger.

What seems like a million clicks later, she's off again to pose in another swimsuit.

She has an incredible figure, which I merely glimpsed last night, and clearly did not fully appreciate as I am doing so now in this intense light. Every sinew of her is perfect, tight, fuckable. Suddenly the urge to be alone with her grips me tight.

She must sense this, as she turns her eyes from the lens and looks directly at me.

And the world just stops.

In this moment there's just her and I.

"I love you," I mouth.

She takes a shuddering breath, eyes still glued on me before the cameraman redirects her attention.

The shoot continues for another hour before she gets a break. It's hard work. It's not about just strutting your stuff. Modelling requires a lot discipline and balance. Some of those poses she was required to undertake took strength and a lot of agility.

"You were amazing," I praise when she snags a bottle of water from me, drinking from it thirstily.

"Thanks, a bit boring for you though."

"Not at all. I could have had worse things to do then watching you get in some of those positions." I wink. "In fact, on some of them I had a bird's eye view."

She bumps me with her water bottle.

"Pervert!"

I hold my hand up. "That's me!"

There's a call. "Shakira, can we go again, this time in the yellow G string?"

She sighs. "No rest for the wicked. You can go if you want, I'll be hauled up here for at least another hour."

I look around. There's six men around this set.

Only two them I have to worry about. But that's still two too many. My mind is already set.

"Nah, it's cool I'll wait."

She gives me a speculative smile, before walking away backwards.

"I love you too, Joey."

My heart leaps into my mouth, the shock of that statement stiffening my muscles. I didn't think she would say it back. It didn't tear me up that she didn't, but I'm tearing up now.

"I think I fell in love with you the first time we met," she continues.

I open my mouth to say something, but nothing comes out. She seems to understand because she gives me that perfect little secretive smile that tells me it's okay.

I keep my eyes trained on her until she disappears into the changing room and it's then a smile curves my own lips.

For the first time in my life, somebody has told me that they love me.

*

I stay with Shakira until the end of the shoot, then take her out to lunch. We didn't talk about what I had said, what she had said. We are good. This relationship isn't about big explanatory statements, it was more about checking in. You ok? You ok? It was easy. I think more so for me we took it as a pace. And I loved that. I love the way she understands me, makes allowances. I promised in my heart right there that I would do the same for her, if she ever needed. I would give her the patience and understanding that she had afforded me so that she could feel her own worth, that she would know, in that moment, I thought about her.

I vowed I would do right by her, make the right decisions, even if that meant ultimately leaving her in order to do so.

*

The next day was interviews day. I was ready in a way that I hadn't been in a long time.

Motivation is the key. And when you don't have any, it means you're in a depression. Which I now accept I was.

It took me a long time to finally admit it. To me admitting it signified one step onto the crazy train that carried my mother as one of their frequent passengers.

And I wasn't ready for that.

But with the help and support of my GP and counsellors, I am now taking a low dose of antidepressants and they are helping to lift my low mood.

I take a last look in the mirror and straighten my back and pull my shoulders back.

"You're ready," I tell my mirror image.

*

I got the job.

I'm now back in employment. Not the same stature at my previous job, but one I'm nonetheless proud to hold.

I have two managers above me. And I'm okay with that, I need safeguards in place.

I'm still in the financial world, still money crunching, but the final decision is not mine, I'm more in an advisory role.

My colleagues know my history, but because I'm not head honcho here, and not in their direct line of fire, they're mostly cool with me. It's good, stable. And for now, I'm happy.

Especially with the way my love life is also shaping up.

Tonight is date night.

Admittedly most nights are now, but we are going to a charity event, so we're like, out- dating.

Not a big deal for me, but it is for Shakira. I'm her first official partner after her husband. A lot of their mutual friends and peers will be attending this charity do, so she's a bit nervous. Understandably so.

I want her to set the tone for tonight, whatever she's comfortable with, I'm happy to step back, forward, even do a go-go dance, anything if that's what's required. I want her to know I support her. How she wants to run this is the way things are going to go.

She's in her bedroom now, trying on dresses and, by the sounds of it, she's getting frustrated.

"Let me see!" I call out from the sitting room.

No answer.

I frown in confusion. "Did you not decide on a dress before now?"

She stomps out of her room and directly to me.

"Do you think that's helpful? Is that why you're here, just to point out the bloody obvious?"

I wince inwardly. Jeez, Louise this woman is going to rip me another backside. I better that the wind out of those sails.

"You look lovely."

She opens her mouth to retaliate, but then realises what I've just said.

"You think?"

"Beautiful, I can't wait to escort you in there. I'll be the envy of them all." And to be fair, even if that statement was a quick-thinking get-out-of-jail-free-card, it was also true. She looked stunning. She had on a midnight-blue floor-length fitted side-split dress that kissed her curves, High open-toes sandals that made her legs look endless, and her naturally wavy hair piled high in a chinion hairdo. She looked delicious.

"Belle of the ball," I emphasised just to drive home the point.

She pivoted around in front of me. "You sure?"

"Absolutely." I kissed my fingers tips. "Bellissimo!"

"That Italian charm, that will always get you out of trouble," she says dryly.

I wink. "I hope so. Listen, you're beautiful anyway, you could turn up in a sack and you will still outdo every woman in the room. Believe me, you're a class act."

She smiles almost shyly. "You're a wonder for my confidence. I think I'll keep you."

"I'm counting on it," I say seriously.

Her breath catches in her throat as I step nearer.

"I've never been happier."

"Me too." She smiles tumultuously.

"I want tonight to be special." I encircle her waist and pull her to me so that our fronts are flush against each other.

She nods.

"This charity night is going to be successful. We are going to raise a lot of money for the Sickle cell society and we are going to raise their organisational profile."

She nods matter of factly at me again.

"And then afterwards … I want to raise something else with you. But in private."

She collapses laughing against me.

I smile. "It's been three months … is that okay? Not moving too fast?"

She gathers herself together and then stretches to kiss me on the lips. "Mr Giovanni, it's more than okay."

I smirk and then slap her arse. "Right let's go raise some money!"

She collects her clutch bag and then we're off.

I'm actually looking forward to the event. I've invited some of my friends, and the guys will be turning up with their partners, so it will be a great opportunity to introduce her to everyone.

When we arrive, there's dozens of people already

there, milling around, drinking champagne, and more importantly viewing the items that are up for the silent auction. One of the items I've contributed is a week sailing on my boat which, by the way, is pretty luxurious.

Another auction up for sale was a private butler for a weekend, which was Gabriel's contribution.

Simon is offering legal services and William, architect planning and drawings. And Jack? … well, he's offering dinner with himself … anyway, there were loads of different offers on the table, and I'm confident we will raise a truck load of money for a very good cause.

"Okay, here we go!" Shakira says, bracing herself and walking forward to introduce me to a long-time friend.

Now, I know I've had my issues, my struggles, but I'm a charming man when I have to be, and especially when I wanted to be, and this was one of those times. I smile, engage, and play my part beautifully, almost naturally, with people who are very important to Shakira. I made sure I wasn't too handsy, too over-the-top, but entertaining, affectionate, and warm. I wanted them to know I respected that this was a change for them all, to see her with another guy. And it was acknowledged, and that it was important to me that I had their approval also.

By their responses it appeared I came across well, if the nodding, approvals smiles, and laughter were anything to go by. I did the whole circle. It seemed everybody was checking me out.

"That was nerve racking!" Shakira said some time later. "I could murder a gin and tonic."

I give her a mock glare, as I know she was joking, and squeezed her hands.

"The initiation is over. I think we're good."

She exhales heavily. "Thank you, that was hard, but you made it so much easier. They see what I see, and they're happy for us."

"Don't shower me with praise yet, you've still got my gang to meet. Just don't judge me by them."

"Ha, if Jack's anything like the rest of them, it's going to be interesting. No, I'm joking, he's a lovely guy, I can't wait to meet the rest of them."

I pull her over immediately and introduce her on mass.

Immediately Alicia and Nicole, Gabriel and William's wives, and also Simon's latest squeeze, Vivienne, spirit her away in order to relay the various tales and misdemeanours that they think our group are responsible for. I hear them giggling loudly and occasional gesturing to us from where they stand.

Gabriel shakes his head. I know for a fact Alicia has got some tall tales to tell. She was telling me she couldn't wait to meet Shakira. He taps his hand on my shoulder. "I'm so sorry man."

I laugh. "If Alicia's is still with you, it can't be all that bad. This won't scare Shakira; believe me, she's seen my ugly."

William smiles. "You really like her, don't you?"

I shake my head. "No, I love her."

That declamation causes them all to pause.

"I thought she was a hook-up," Jack eventually blurts out.

I laugh, it's ironic, especially since we hadn't even had sex. But then that's our business. I look Jack square in the eye.

"She's no hook-up, she's my girl."

I step closer to him, and take his hand. "But you will always hold a special place in my heart too."

He smirks and pushes me away.

When the girls return there's an easy camaraderie between all of us, and it's like we've all known each other for ages. I feel for the first time, a sense of belonging.

The silent auction was a roaring success, we raised thousands for the sickle cell organisation and Shakira gave a wonderful speech, thanking everyone for their participation. It was then that she mentioned me, and I was asked to stand up in recognition for my unwavering support. It moved me. I looked in her eyes, and in front of everyone, I told her that I loved her. The audience cooed and clapped, but such was the intensity of feeling between us at that very moment, I noticed no one.

After the speeches, the chairs and tables were removed and there was dancing.

Now I love to dance. You'd think I would look funny busting some moves at my height, 6'5 – but I don't. You see I'm not lanky and awkward. I know what my long limbs are doing. And believe me, they're in coordination.

So I had a great time. I danced all night, didn't sit down. I felt carefree. On top of the world. I didn't even miss the glass I would normally be holding while partying. Didn't miss the random girl who would attach to me, hoping for free drinks and a bunk up after. Didn't miss it one bit.

My eyes, my body, my heart, and my sanity belonged to just one person.

Shakira.

Chapter 12

We're kissing. We just got out of the cab, and I'm fumbling blindly looking for my front door key.

I should detach for a second, make this process easier – but I can't. So it takes three times as long to get into the bloody house. Just as I'm about to kick the door shut behind us, I hear a voice. A familiar one. A slurring one. One that is capable of sending shivers down my spine.

I freeze.

That voice has the same reaction on me like a nail on a blackboard.

I hate it.

Shakira reacts first. She steps in front of me,

almost like a shield. She senses there's something wrong, and the perceived threat is the one that is swaying unsteadily now in front of us.

But I won't let her take a bullet for me, so I gently take her hand and guide her behind me.

"Hello, mum."

She laughs. Her voice robbed of its former femininity, is now lower, raspier.

"JoJo, come give mummy a kiss, it's been a long time."

Shakira's frame jerks against me. She remembers. Teasing me one time, she called me JoJo. She didn't realise. Now I know that she will never call me that name again. I squeeze her hand. it's alright, I'm assuring her, you didn't know.

I answer my mother now. "What do you want?"

She looks at me with reproach, as if she doesn't like my tone.

"I need a place to stay. I got kicked out."

I lift my chin. "What did you do with the money I sent?"

"Fucking three thousand pounds? Is that what a millionaire sends his mother? How long was that supposed to last?"

"The month."

"Well it fucking didn't."

"Too bad, I can't help you this time." I move to shut the door. But she's faster, and her dirty nails are wrapped around the edge.

"One night, that's all I'm asking for! You used to let me stay. For fucks sakes I'm your mum!"

Pain. Anger, but most of all embarrassment wells up inside me. And against my will, I feel my self-protective walls spring up and slam into place. I never wanted Shakira to see me like this. See *her*. Because it's all so ugly, and so damn awful. I am the product of *this*.

"Go in the sitting room," I instruct Shakira.

"No, I'm staying."

I raise my voice. "GO!"

She startles, and then retreats. I can sense her hurt, rejection, but I only seek to protect her, not only from mum, but from me too.

My mum smiles. She's missing several front teeth. The rest of them black, rotten, a stinking mess. I can smell the rest of her too, it's all I can do not to heave.

"I love you, JoJo."

My blood turns cold. "I need you to go," I say it calmly, too calmly considering the chaos that's currently going on inside my head.

"Just a few days, son, until I get sorted. Then I'll leave you and your bit of skirt alone. Was I interrupting? Never mind, you can carry on, I'm not bothered."

Revulsion pools in my stomach, and for a second I think I'm going to throw up.

This woman is my mother. I should love her, honour her, but all I feel is twisted hate, and deep, deep unassailable shame. My heart is hammering, chest visibly heaving.

Mum laughs. She knows she has the upper hand and is revelling in it. She can render me powerless, useless, just by the mere sight of her. She knows all of this.

"JoJo, come on JoJo, let mummy stay." She moves nearer. I take a step back.

She clicks her tongue tauntingly.

"Still weak. Pathetic. You take after him, and not me in that regard." She nods her head in the direction Shakira went. "She will find that out too, and she will leave your arse. She's headstrong that girl, I could tell that from the second I saw her. Trouble. She's probably after your money, that's what this is. The minute she's got enough, she'll be gone, and you'll be plotless." She exhales heavily, and I throw up a little in my mouth. The smell, it's a mixture of stale alcohol, halitosis, and just plan rot. It's disgusting.

As I look at her, I feel a sudden shift change happen. The axis tilts. I'm detached, almost robotic. There is only so much a person can take, and I've reached my uppermost limit.

"So, what do you say, eh? Two days, two days to get myself sorted. I know you don't want to see me out on the street." She smiles, a persuasive smile, if you count a hyena's smile as so.

"I don't care where you go, but you're not staying

here." There is no affliction in my tone, it's almost as if I've flatlined.

The vile smile is wiped from my mother's face instantly.

"What?"

"This is the last time I'm going to say this. Turn around and go."

She frowns, like I'm talking another language.

And it must seem that way, because I've always given in. Why? Because she is my mother, and as much as I hate how she's treated me, it's inbuilt that it's what you do. You help your mother. Not anymore though, that shit is over. I hate her, every part of her, every bone.

Brilliant green eyes, still curiously vibrant, widen incredulously and I witness the twisted change.

"I should have offed you, the moment I realised I was pregnant. That man you call your father persuaded me otherwise. I should have known he would raise a weakling, a good-for-nothing selfish prick. At least if I had stayed with your sperm donor,

I would have had a more exiting life, but no, I had to pick the sensible one, the boring one, and look how that had turned out!"

My insides are wound up like a clockwork mechanism ready to go off while on the outside my eyes burn with hatred.

"Don't look at me like that! You think you're any better than me? Ha," she laughs. "I've seen you, I've seen you in the bars." She puts her face right up close to mine. "You're a drunk with money. That's the only difference between us."

I swallow hard. That hurt. Right where it was supposed to. I stand still, waiting for the tirade to finish, all the while knowing I'm building inside like a volcano.

"It's a pity that you can't show me more respect in front of your girlfriend … or is that what this is about? Is she the reason why you've suddenly grown some balls? why I'm not getting any money? She needs to be careful; I can arrange for her pretty little face to get rearranged." She shrugs. "Wouldn't take much."

Something pops in my brain. I don't want her

here. I don't want her to talk anymore. I don't want her even to take another breath …

"Joseph!"

I swing around startled, and my hand drops back to my side.

Shakira stands there. Her expression one of anguish.

"I'll call the police," she warns my mother. "Go now."

My mother eyes flare through mine. She expects me to defend her. Even now, she expects respect because she birthed me. I step back. My hands at my sides still bunched. I am fighting for self-control.

Shakira gets out her mobile.

And my mum knows she's lost.

"Twenty pounds," she begs, her voice less authoritarian now.

"Not a penny," Shakira refuses.

My mother let's rip. Before she's done she insults Shakira's race, her looks, even her clothes, damming her as one of my prostitutes. And once again, more disturbingly, she threatens her with physical violence.

The scene is ugly, ugly.

And I failed to protect her.

"I'm sorry that happened," I say dully. I've gone numb.

"It wasn't your fault." Shakira takes a step towards me.

I retreat. I don't want to hurt her, but I can't bear that she is here now. I feel dirty, not worthy.

"Joe?" I hear her uncertainty.

"Look, it's late, I'll call you a taxi."

"No, don't you dare check out on me now!" she says, her voice rising.

"I'll call you tomorrow."

"You will talk to me today!"

I look at her, she's so angry. Reminds me on the night we first met. An angry, beautiful, pissed-off warrior.

"Shakira …" I shake my head. She deserves so much more.

"Don't do this, Joe, I need you." Her voice trembles.

I hate to see her cry. I had resolved never to make her cry, no matter how unrealistic that was in reality.

I reach out and tuck a strand of hair behind her ears.

"I wish you hadn't seen that," I whisper.

"She's your mum, Joe, she's supposed to love you. It's not your fault she's sick."

"That woman, she makes me …" My voice cracks.

Shakira holds my face.

"I was going to hit her," I tell her mournfully. "Make everything stop." The realisation reaffirms everything in me I already know.

She shakes her head. "No."

I nod my head. "Yes, you saw it. I was going to hurt her."

"You wouldn't have, in the end. You're not that guy, Joe."

I laugh, but without humour.

Shakira drops her hands and we stand there like

strangers. The silence between us is palpable.

"Would like a drink, Joe?" she says suddenly, almost conversationally.

My eyes jerks to hers.

What?

"Because I do. Right now. I feel like a large glass of red. Or maybe some gin. I could murder some gin right now." She buttons up her coat.

My mouth is agape. "What are you doing?"

"I'm doing what you're doing, I'm giving up. I'm going to the off-licence, and I'm going to get sloshed. Coming?"

"That's not funny."

"No, it's not, is it? But that's exactly what I'm going to do anyway." She moves to leave.

I grab her arm. "Don't!"

"Why Joe, why not?" she challenges.

My nostrils flare. "Because it's not worth it."

"You, or the drink?" she taunts.

I close my eyes. I wanted so badly to undo the last

ten minutes, just wipe it out.

"I needed a minute," I confess. "To reset. My mother has the ability to disable me like no one else … except you. You two are my Achilles heel. One Kryptonite, the other, life blood. The Kryptonite will kill me, the life blood will save me."

"You know the thing with Kryptonite, Joe? You stay away from it and it can't hurt you. Get an injunction. Cut all ties. You don't have to put up with it. No more money, no more place to stay. No more nothing. You are not responsible for her."

"You think she's going to just disappear? That an injunction can stop a woman who doesn't have anything to lose? At least the money keeps her at bay."

"For how long? The more you give, the more she'll want."

"I'd give her everything, if it meant not seeing her again."

Shakira rubs my back. "It's got to stop, Joe."

"I know." I turn into her. "I'll never let her hurt you again."

She shakes her head. "She didn't. She's a mess, I'm worried about you, us, what this can do to us."

"Did you mean it about the drink?" I ask abruptly.

"No, I just wanted to snap you out of it."

"It worked."

"Then lean on me, don't push me away, that hurt."

I nod my acknowledgement. "I don't feel like a man when she's near. I feel like a kid. A frightened kid. It's hard for me to let you see that, you can do so much better."

"I want you!" she insists. "I love you!"

"I longed for those words for so long, that sometimes they don't feel real." I sigh. "Why does she hate me so much? Why couldn't she love me?"

"Because she's ill, and she's too far gone now to change. You have to accept that. Maybe once, a long time ago, she was different, but alcohol can affect the chemicals in your mind, and sometimes you don't get back. Perhaps your father was hoping … I don't know, but you can't spend your time doing that anymore. She's gone, and you're never going to glimpse the woman she once was. You have to forge another ending. One that's happy and hopeful, and without her. She doesn't define you."

I exhale heavily. "I fucked up. All of this counselling and I've gone back to square one."

"No, you don't suddenly become a maverick. It will take time. But piece by piece, the connection is made. Hang on in there."

"Just as long as you're beside me." I desperately search her eyes.

"I'm right beside you," she assures, tucking her hand in mine.

I lift her hand and bring it to my lips. "Thank you." Together we walk into the sitting room and I don't get two feet before I wince audibly.

I forgot.

She gives a small smile. "It's lovely. A little inappropriate right now, but the execution, brilliant."

I look around. There are dozens of flowers beautifully arranged in glass vases. The aroma, incredible. Floating candles also adorned the room alongside a roaring fire. Champagne, chocolates. I had arranged for this to be done when we were at the charity event so that it was ready the moment we stepped in.

My attempt at seduction.

Ruined.

"I don't feel jiggy right now," I confess.

She laughs. "For a man that used to sleep with different girls most nights, I'm finding it incredibly hard to get my leg over!"

I smile. "You're not just some girl. You're special."

She stretches up and kisses me softly on the lips.

"It can wait – everything has its time. I won't say no to a cuddle though."

I swallow the lump in my throat. I absolutely adore this girl.

"Let's go up."

We walk up the stairs together, her head tucked into the crook of my neck.

We undress, I turn down the covers of the bed.

We get in, snuggle together.

Exhausted.

I need a resolution.

Shakira's right. Everything has its time. This cannot go on, and I won't let her destroy us. I know my mum; I saw it in her eyes. I know she'll come for Shakira next. Anything to get to me. She won't forgive leaving without the money, and Shakira was the catalyst to that.

My mum knows so many shady characters, I can't afford to take any chances. The people she associates with would maim a person for a pound.

I pretend to sleep, fooling my girlfriend, whilst all the while, I plot the downfall of my mother.

Shakira would be shocked, but I know while I have changed in a whole manner of ways, in this I have not.

Survival.

The instinct is kicking in again. The dark side. And this time I won't try to suppress it.

If it's between Shakira and my mum, my mum will lose.

*

The next day, Sunday, we kick back, read the papers in bed, eat too much of what is bad for us. It's relaxed. Normal. Good Joe is here. He's making everything chilled, creating a scene of domestication.

However, inside, I am angry, finally reaching my end point.

Nobody threatens mine.

I was too young to protect my father.

But I am a man now.

And I will protect Shakira at all cost.

Chapter 13

I know she hangs out here. This place is dank, squalid, and disused. Her kind of place.

I push the tin-like door and gain access. There are people here … well bodies on the floor anyway, all strung out. I don't know if they're alive or dead, and I don't care much either, my only mission is to find her. And then deal with her.

I had told Shakira that I was popping out to see Simon about something. So I have time. For his part, Simon will cover my back. He may be a solicitor by profession, but he's also a man of the world, and he understands some things just need to be done.

Out of all my friends he knows what happened to me. Some anyway. The rest is too terrible to recount and remains buried within.

And that's where it will remain.

I only wanted her to love me, and now she's driven me to do this. There's no turning back, I will finish this today. If I get caught then I will go to prison and sit there knowing I did right. Shakira will hurt, but she will know as much that I did it for her, and in doing so, I did my best.

I hitch the duffel bag I carry more securely around my shoulder and take a left up the narrow stairs where more bodies are draped. I step over them like they're bags of rubbish, their stench, unbelievable.

I recount another smell from a long time ago. One of burning flesh.

My dad's.

She once threw boiling hot water over him. He wouldn't give her more housekeeping, knowing it would go on drink. She was furious. He covered it up, said he had slipped in a bath of hot water, but I had seen everything. I remember crying, and him telling me not to worry because it didn't hurt. But it must have done. Terribly.

He didn't go to hospital. Now I know it was to protect her.

I hate this woman.

I reach the top of the stairs and turn left. There's a narrow corridor and then after that more stairs. This place is like an empty warehouse. Looks much smaller on the outside, but there's a warren of rooms.

Which one is she in?

That takes me back to a game I enjoyed when I was younger. Hide and go seek. Me and my two friends Dorothy and Craig were playing.

Mum was out. She had gone missing a couple of days earlier, and the house was peaceful.

My dad had been worried sick, but I prayed she would never come back. He went looking for her anyway, told us to play nicely until he got back.

It was my turn to hide.

I was feeling smug, I had found a good place. In the laundry room, just behind the giant boiler. Nobody liked to come in here, for it was really hot, plus a little creepy, and there was only a shard of light coming from one side window. I was confident they would give up and I would win the game.

Then I heard a sound. Shuffling footsteps. Didn't sound like Dorothy or Craig's. I was confused. Then I heard a hiccup. And I knew it was her. Dear god she was back. My heart plummeted, and then kicked right back up. I was alone down here. With her.

Not a good position to be in.

I held my breath, kept as still as a statue.

But she has a missile-type beam, and she locked straight down on her target.

"Get out here!" she screams. "You think I can't see you? I can see your big foot. That's what I'm going to call you from now. 'Big foot Yeti'." She laughs.

Reluctantly I reveal myself. She comes straight towards me and slaps me hard around the face.

"Don't ever hide from me again," she slurs.

"But I was hiding from—"

She slaps me again, this time harder. "Don't answer me back!" she spits.

I clamp my mouth shut, trembling.

"Do you know what they do with boys that are rude to their mothers?"

I shake my head, fright now seizing me up.

"They make them parade in their underpants with a sign."

I shake my head again, more vigorously.

"No, not that. Dorothy and Craig are here."

"Strip."

"Please mum—"

Another slap.

Slowly, as if giving her time to change her mind, I start to take off my clothes, until finally I'm just in my briefs.

She gets out a felt tip pen and writes on my chest BASTARD.

I don't know what it means, but I already know I'm ashamed.

She then hits me again and again. Never on my face, body blows.

I withstand it as much as I can, only whimpering a little. I'm desperate that my friends don't hear.

But that's not good enough for her, she likes to hear my pain.

She takes a cigarette out of her bag and lights it.

I'm afraid. Really afraid. This is really going to hurt. I beg her no, which just seems to spur her on. Slowly she taunts me with it.

I beg her again. I'm so frightened I feel a trickle between my legs.

She stops and looks down. A smile comes on her face.

She then calls my friends, telling them she's found me ...

*

There's a reason I'm recounting. My practical side is in full affect. It's preparation. It's enabling me to do this. I can't afford to be sentimental and reasoning, I will never be able to do this otherwise.

I have to empty my love for her completely.

I get to the top of the stairs. And I hear faint

moaning.

Sounds like her.

I push open the door and step in, more cautious now who might be in here.

She's alone and strung out. Not only is my mum an alcoholic, drugs have now been added to her repertoire.

Perfect.

I stop in front of her. She cranes her neck from her slumped position, her expression at first anxious, but then, as she realises it's me, mocking. She smiles.

Bold.

Even now she thinks she's going to win.

"Marie." I cannot bear to call her mum.

She frowns, just a tiny bit, not used to my lack of respect.

"JoJo!" she crones. "What have you brought mama?"

I can see she's not well. She's lying in an awkward position, literally a 35 degree angle. If that wall wasn't there, she would be flat on her back.

I stoop down.

"Lots of things."

She gives a toothless grin. Jesus, someone's knocked out the remaining ones she had last night. My stomach turns.

I unzip the bag I've carried with me and she practically sticks her head into it.

Desperation is a graceless thing.

"Where's the money?" she questions gruffly.

"I've brought you something better. You don't have to go out at all to get what you want; I've brought it here for you instead."

Hesitation.

Because she knows, whilst I like a drink, I abhor drugs.

Her eyes narrow. "Why did you do that?"

I begin to zip the bag up. "Well if you don't want it …"

Her mucky fingers are already preventing my progress.

"I didn't say that!" she amends quickly.

I nod and place the bag beside her.

She dips in and takes out the speedball, pure cocaine, one of the deadliest.

She holds it aloft like a proud mother holding a child. I'm surprised she's not licking her lips.

I nod at the bag. "There's other stuff in there too." I'm talking about the Xanax, Prozac, Co-codamol, speed.

My pharmacist friend has served me well.

"Have you brought some drink as well?"

Greedy bitch. She's never satisfied.

I pull a can of special brew out of the bag.

"I got this for you."

She snatches it out of my hands, snaps the ring pull back and drinks thirstily.

'That's my girl,' I say in my head. 'Down the hatch.'

Suddenly she stops.

"Aren't you having some?" She's still slightly suspicious.

But I've come prepared. I pull out another can. And swallowing the lump in my throat, I take a gulp.

Up to now I've gone months without a drop to my lips.

But desperate situations call for desperate measures, and I cannot afford for my plan to go array.

The instant the liquid eats my stomach, I get a welcome home cheer. But I'm stronger than that. I'm now captain of my own destiny and the compass is pointing due north to recovery.

This won't derail me.

She wipes her hands across her mouth, apparently satisfied I'm a fallen solider now and carries on drinking her can.

"Wait," I say. "Surely you're going to have some of what I've brought you first. You'll need to save some of that drink to wash it down with."

Again, she pauses. My mother is no fool, unfortunately for her though, her habit, her need, is greater.

She takes the tablets first, not caring what they are,

stuffing them into her mouth whilst she prepares all the stuff to enable her to smoke the cocaine.

She's an expert at this, even half strung. Pity she wasn't as adept at feeding me food when I was younger.

"Want some?" Bizarrely she exhibits some manners.

I look at her, disgust barely concealed. "You're too kind. No, you have it all." I check myself; I cannot afford the bite. I need to rein it in. I smile.

"I had some already."

"Cool." She seems happy enough with my explanation and lights the pipe.

It doesn't take long. A few drags and she's drooping evermore sideways.

I stand there and watch for a few seconds, curiously detached before casually sliding down the wall into a sitting position next to where her head is now positioned.

I understand hearing is the last sense to go, and I need her to hear this.

"I want to tell you that I hate you," I say to her

conversationally. "Hate how you treated me, my dad, and even what you were planning for Shakira. You know, my whore.

"So you understand that this, right here, has to happen. I must confess though, that part of me found aspects of this hard, what with you being my mother and all, but I've found a way to circumnavigate that. You see, I've pretended that my mother had died. A long time ago. So really, you don't actually exist now, and this isn't actually happening."

I hear a faint moan from her, but I press on.

"As for slating my birthright yesterday? I don't give two fucks who my biological sperm donor is or was. That men Franco Francis Giovanni was my father. And I will acknowledge him only. So fail there too.

"I now have purpose in my life, I have a woman that I love and who loves me, despite me being so repulsive as you'd have me believe. Oh yeah, and by the way, I no longer drink – and I definitely don't do drugs. I prefer to get high on life instead. As a matter of fact, I'm the happiest now that I've ever been." I lean down real close to her ear.

"So you lose mama. You didn't destroy me, you only made little JoJo stronger in the end. And I will survive this, I will survive you. So, close your heavy eyes now, and never wake up, because there is no point, no one loves you and no one will come looking for you this time."

I hear her gurgle, and then give some short breaths. I believe the term is agonal breathing and I realise she's well on her way out.

I don't have to stay. She's not getting up from this.

I collect my bag, brush down my trousers, and walk out without even a glance back.

It's over.

Chapter 14

"Hi hon, I've changed the bedsheets and put on fresh linen. How was Simon?" Shakira leans over to kiss me and I jerk back abruptly.

Fuck, I forgot the mouthwash.

Shakira double blinks. "Have I done someone wrong?" she asks in a small, worried voice.

I laugh nervously. "No. I ate some garlic bread at Simon's, I'm self-conscious about that sort of thing."

"Oh," she looks nonplussed. "Well, I guess we're still learning about each other."

I smile tightly, keeping my jaws together and slip into the bathroom.

I emerge seconds later, minty fresh from the

alcohol I drank in order to act out my charade.

I feel no pleasure lying to Shakira.

None at all.

I've just aided in the demise of my mother, so this is a necessity.

"Should I start dinner?" I enquire breezily.

"Didn't you just snack?" She teases. "Honestly you're like a Gannett."

"It was only a couple of slices," I lie.

"So, did you manage to solve your little problem Simon was helping you with?" she asks, slipping on a bar stool at my kitchen island.

I blanch slightly. "Yes, it's finally resolved."

"Good," she replies happily. "So I've got your full attention?

I look at her square on. "You've always got my full attention."

"Okkkay. Well, I've done something naughty."

I forced a smile. "What have you done?"

"I've booked us a holiday. Well, more like a long

weekend actually. I think it will relax us, and then maybe then we can get to the next stage?" she asks almost shyly.

I look regretfully at her. "Last night was a nightmare."

"Yes, it was. But we won't dwell on that. We'll just keep it moving. At least we won't get disturbed on this break. Unless of course she decides to stalks us." She barks out a laugh, before noting my expression. She apologises immediately.

"Bad timing. Guess we're not at that stage yet?"

I rub my fingers over my eyes. "No, not quite."

She winches slightly. "Still up for going away though?"

I look up to her, a small smile now pulling up my lips. "Absolutely."

"It's going to be alright, Joe. You'll see, everything will work out the way it's supposed to. But you have to face up to your mum, the situation will not change until you put things in place."

"I've already done it, that's why I went to see

Simon. He's put out an injunction."

"I'm glad. As you said she'll probably oppose it, but there are consequences if she does. It was the right thing to do."

"It was the only thing to do. It stops now."

"I'm so proud of you."

I feel sick. I momentarily close my eyes. 'Deep breath,' I coach myself. Don't break now.

"Veggies or salad?" I say now, brightly.

"Any," Shakira answers cheerfully. "Hey, you still haven't asked where we're going!"

"No, I haven't, have I? Sorry, where are you whisking me off to?"

"Ok, it's still in England, guess."

I love her, but I haven't got the stomach for this right now.

"Come on, give it up." I widen my eyes, I try and appear playful while all the while the adrenaline is building in me.

"No spoilsport! Guess."

I take an inward breath, trying not to show any aggravation.

"I can't think when I'm hungry!" I jokingly complain.

"Oh you're not fun! Lake Windermere!"

"What?"

"The Lake Windermere, your favourite place! I want you to teach me to fish, I want us to go on long walks, I want to see the place you love through your eyes."

I feel moisture at the back of my eyes, and my breath stutters. This is what love is. Shakira.

Shakira is love.

I nod my head, unable to speak. "Thank you," I manage to get out at last.

She climbs of the stool and comes beside me, wrapping her arms around my waist.

"We're gonna make it, Joey. Through all of this. Just me and you."

I lean against her, burying my face in her silky hair. Its soft fragrance calming me immediately. "I'm going to make you feel my love every day," I promise her.

"Know this. Every action is because I love you. Never doubt that."

She pulls away and searches my eyes. Deep understanding passes through.

She gets it. She knows there's layers to me, layers that she can't possibly understand, but she's choosing to support me, even if the decisions I make are difficult and impactful on her.

"I trust you, Joe. With all my being. Just try to come home to me is all I ask."

I kiss her lips. "You are my home, and I will always find my way. I love you Shakira. I love you all the world."

*

The police visited a few days later. They needed me to identify the body.

I played my part well but didn't feel the need to come over as the distressed son. Everyone knew by now what she was, how she lived, and when something happens like that, there's an element of predictability. So, you have to be upset – but there's no need to thump and wail.

Walking in that cold sterile room at the morgue, I felt nothing. It was just something that needed to be done. A tick box exercise if you like.

They lifted the covers and I looked at her for the last time. Shakira squeezed my hands, and I dutifully squeezed back, but there was nothing.

"That's her," I say dully.

They nodded and covered her back up, and then I turned and walked out.

*

"Do you want us to stop for some coffee?" Shakira asks worriedly. "You probably need some sugar."

"No, I um, I have to get back to work. I've missed some meetings and it's going to be hell to catch up."

Shakira double blinked. "You're not going back to work now, surely not!"

"I'm alright, Shakira, I just need to keep busy."

'Of course, of course, I'm sorry, it's just that you don't have you rush, it's quite a shock you've had today."

"Yeah, sure, but I'll be okay." I hope I've used the right dilation of tone.

"I'm gonna cancel the holiday."

I stop still. "What! No, we need this. We both need to get away, a lot has happened in such a short space of time, we need to focus on us."

Shakira sighs. "I don't know how you're coping; it worries me."

I lift her chin up and look in her eyes. "As long as I've got you, I can cope with anything. Look, you know that my mother and I weren't close. This situation is … difficult. Of course, it's feels off, my mum is dead – but I'm not going to pretend I'm devastated. It was just a matter of time before what happened, happened anyway."

"I know, but still … despite everything …"

"I'm okay sweetheart, really," I insist. "I just need a break, I need to kickback for a while, and so do you, we both deserve this."

Shakira thinks for a few seconds before giving a resigned smile. "Okay, big guy, we'll go. You're right, it'll probably help getting away."

"Definitely," I agree. I give Shakira a quick peck on the cheek and we separate, whilst she goes to catch the tube home, I head back to work. I walked the rest of the way in a trance. Numb, detached. I don't remember the route; only inbuilt familiarity ensures that I reach there.

When I walk in, I do not tell my colleagues that my mum was dead, and that this very morning I had been identifying her body, I carry on just as if I had just been to a dental appointment. I check the Dow Jones, chair two meetings, even sit in on an interview – as calm as anything. To all extents and purposes, it's simply a normal day. It did bother me, however, that I had no definite feelings about what I had just done. But as soon as that thought threatened to become overwhelming, I dismissed it out of hand. I had a route that I was determined to stick to, sentimentality never won the day. Besides, I was used to suffering, one more thing to add to the list was neither here nor there to me. That night, after I visited my mum, I had slept. All the way through. I had even woken the next

morning and had initially forgotten what I had done –
until Shakira had mentioned something about my
mum, and then it had all come flooding back. Sure, at
first, when returning home, I had been antsy, but I
had settled. Rebooted. It was over.

Of course there is a risk I could still get found out
and go to prison for the rest of my life. But it was a
low risk. Crack houses rarely gartered the precious
resources of an already overworked police force, and
it was accepted she had died because of an overdose,
why would they start looking for suspects?

No, what I needed to be more concerned about
was what this whole scenario said about me. What I
was capable of, and how emotionless I was at doing
this deed – and then shaking it off.

I suppose I didn't consider myself a murderer,
more an enabler. It was a fine line, and not one that
would stand up to scrutiny in any decent society, but
one I could live with all the same.

So, I dismissed it all and did what I told my
mother I would do; I pretended she had died a long
time ago, and the last week simply hadn't happened.

I was good with that.

*

The next week we packed my car and took turns driving to Lake Windermere.

It was nice having a driving partner so I could actually see the landscape instead of just the lonely road ahead of me.

I looked out of the window like a tourist. I could tell Shakira enjoyed watching that side of me also. I was carefree, more accessible. Also, I talked more when I was comfortable.

I told her about my father, how he introduced me to fly fishing. The hours we spent at the riverbank, eating our sandwiches in companionable silence. The walks through the woods, sometimes the bramble in there cutting into my legs. But I hadn't cared, I was with my dad and that's was all that mattered.

It's easy to think of my dad just as a victim, he withstood a lot of abuse from my mum. But in the end he chose to stay, it was his decision to try and reach her somehow. I'm certain he never imaged things would turn out the way they did, that she would outlive him and I would be subjected to that. I'm certain of it. He did his best for me, even in retrospect that would have been to leave her, and take me with him.

But I don't hold that against him. To me my dad was my hero. He was certainly more adjusted than I.

On the drive, I managed to tease out some of Shakira's life with her husband David.

It seemed that both of them had had a love of travel, and although it was obvious she was still incredibly angry with him, which enviably coloured some of her responses, it was also clear that they had clearly loved each other very much and had been looking forward to a promising future together.

And I don't begrudge that.

Not one little bit.

I don't feel possessive of their love. She has every right to love a man that, excluding one tiny moment, albeit life-changing, had done right by her.

I actually wish that she could forgive him, or at

least let it go. But I knew that the anger she was holding onto was the only thing sustaining her. If she accepted what happened she would be forced to deal with her grief, and she wasn't ready for that. Not yet.

So I will keep chipping away until she's ready to open up her grief, and I will be here for her absolutely when she does.

Chapter 15

The cottage where we were staying was essentially a fisherman's shack. Rustic, characterful, and quite basic. It had only one bedroom, one bathroom, and a small living area with coal fire.

It was perfect.

"You chose well," I compliment her.

She winked. "I know my man."

And she did. It was just what I would have chosen. Together we were a good fit.

We walked in, dumped our suitcases, and immediately put the old kettle on the fire to heat up.

"You know alcohol is all well and fine, but you can't beat a good cup of tea!" she joked.

"That's true." I agree. "Tea, it's part of the fabric in these parts. I can't imagine being drunk while I was here. Alcohol and the great outdoors doesn't go somehow."

"Do you crave it?"

I waggle my eyebrows. "Just what are we talking about here?"

"No silly," she giggles. "The great outdoors. It certainly beats sitting in a stuffy office all day looking at figures."

I smile. "It does, but I also enjoy what I do. I'm toying with combining the two actually. Open up a business similar to the facilities here. With fishing rights, boating, rambling. A feel-good back-to-nature reserve."

She gasps. "That's an excellent idea! You would be in your element!"

"Yeah I would. Not really your bag though?"

Shakira grins uppishly. "I wait to be persuaded."

"Well that's a challenge I'd be willing to accept."

"Come on," Shakira says excitedly, "let's get this

tea drunk and get out there and explore."

Crazy happy at her enthusiasm, I quickly finish my tea, and start gathering the fish rods and tackle. We walk to the jetty, hire a paddling boat, and then oar into a prime position. I decide it's best to string the tackle for the both of us when I catch sight of Shakira's expression following the opening of the bait, and then I teach her to cast off.

So we sit there for a while, me blissful, Shakira wiggling. I try not to laugh. She's trying, she really is, but it's a fact. Some people find fishing boring.

I turn to her, and she gives me a false smile, and then I burst out laughing.

"You're hating this, aren't you?"

"No, no," she answers in an unnaturally high voice. She sees my expression. "Okay, it's mind-numbingly, excruciatingly, boring!" she bursts out.

I literally double back, barking out my laughter, and frightening the fish.

"Well, at least that's honest!"

She groans. "I'm so sorry, do you hate me?"

I gather her shoulders to me and hug her. "Completely! No, don't be silly, it's quite healthy to have different hobbies, besides, I will never catch anything with the way you fidget!"

She slaps me playfully, then lets out a piercing scream.

It startles me until I realise she's got a pull on her line. I quickly straighten up.

"Okay relax, don't tug against it, just hold it straight."

Shakira is still screaming, going completely loopy.

"Hold it straight!" I shout out.

"I'm trying, you big oaf, I'm trying!" she yells.

"Wheel it in, come on, quickly!" I say, trying to grab the line and help her.

She shrugs me away. "Let me do it!" She jumps up.

"Careful!" I shout as the small boat rocks precariously.

"I've nearly got him!" she screams, jumping up and down.

Then the enviable happens.

We tip over.

*

"My hair has seaweed in it," she sulks ten minutes later when we manage to clamber back on to the boat and row it back to the bank.

"This isn't the sea," I remind her as we walk back to the cabin, dripping wet.

"It smells!"

"Okay we'll jump in the shower and I will wash it for you."

She stops dead. "We?"

I turn to her. "We," I say firmly. "I haven't been so turned on since I was in the sixth year. All that flapping around in the water. I must like mermaids or something."

Shakira's mouth is ajar. "I look like a drowned rat!"

"You look beautiful," I correct her

A smile creeps on her lips. "Race you back!" She

suddenly comes alive, her limbs nubile and ready.

I drop the kit and set after her, both of us running for all we're worth back to the cabin.

She gets there a second before me and tries to slam the cabin door shut before I get in.

But my strength supersedes her, and I easily wrestle the door back open.

She backs away. Slowly retreating, the dare in her eyes saying, 'Come get me'.

And I duly do so. My soft tread almost stalking her progress.

"Take them off," I demand.

Her eyes flare slightly at my tone. "Take what off?" she questions coyly.

"Your clothes. Take. Them. Off."

"Yes sir," she murmurs as she slowly hitches her sodden jumper over her head. The jumper, saturated with water, weighs a ton, making it difficult, and her head gets tangled in the neck.

I have to go over to help her, and I get tangled in it as well, adding to the confusion.

Sexy, this is not.

"Oh, sod this for a game of soldiers!" she declares, stripping the rest of her clothes off with more speed than grace.

She stands there, naked, proud, and pissed off, and she looks majestic.

"Am I allowed to say wow, or will you berate me?"

She cools down a little. "Wow is ok."

"Then wow!"

"Your turn," she says, her chest heaving.

I start to strip off, a little slower than she, unable to take my eyes off of her. She's absolutely perfect. High pert small breasts, reed-flat stomach, shapely flare hips, and legs that go on for miles.

I then realise she's staring nervously at me.

"I haven't done this in a long time," she says quickly.

I look down. I'm not a small guy, in any way, and I'm probably scaring her.

"I'm not going to hurt you; we'll take it real slow," I assure her.

I watch her gulp. "Real slow," she reiterates.

I stretch my hand and she walks towards me. I lean down and give her the softest of kisses.

"Mmm, that's nice," she hums appreciatively. I then edge down and lightly nip her on the neck.

"But that's even better."

I chuckle and scoot down to hoist her into my arms. "I know the perfect place to take this." I say, shouldering the bedroom door open and drop her on to the bed.

She screams. The bed is as hard as nails. The springs, broken and twisted.

"Fucking hell!" I exclaim. "Shakira I'm so sorry."

She hankers to her side, rubbing her backside.

"Is this fate or is there something bloody wrong with us?"

"Don't worry, I have an idea." I gather some blankets and some pillows and go arrange them near the fireplace in the front room.

It doesn't take me long to get the fire started, and hey presto we had a magical setting.

"My hero."

"Come here," I invite throatily, she walks over then kneels down beside me.

We kiss like mad and melt into each other and for the rest of the night we remain there, finally cementing our relationship, making love all night.

*

"What do you think about babies?"

"Three. I want three," she says definitively.

I smile in the darkness.

"What about you?" she says when I give no response.

"Didn't want them, afraid they would turn out like me, you know, carry the gene."

"Oh." She sounds disappointed.

"But now I'm thinking, three is a nice number."

"Really?"

"Yeah, but one of them has to be a boy, I have to have someone to go fishing with!"

"Meh, okay."

"And the girls have to look like you."

She laughs. "Deal. I love you, Joseph, really love you."

"I love you too sweetheart."

The end

Epilogue

So we lived happy ever after …

Well, not quite.

Because this is no fairytale.

Alcohol is a powerful beast, and once you opened the door to that beast, it's so dammed hard to kick it out again.

Shakira, out of the two of us, was the most resilient. Yes, once or twice she was severely tested, but she managed not to succumb.

I wasn't so fortunate.

I mean, I basically killed my own mother, right?

You don't do that and then get to live in unparalleled happiness.

And there's something right about that. You shouldn't. No matter what.

Two months after that event, I broke down.

Drank like a sailor.

Shakira left me.

It was what she was supposed to do. It was our agreement. The right thing to do.

But it broke me.

I thought I would go mad.

It was, however, the start of my recovery again. I couldn't bear the loss of her, so I was forced to seek help.

I hauled my arse back to rehab and that forthright, interfering, brilliant nurse put me together, again.

And now we're back together and taking it slow. I have to rebuild what I tore down.

Part of that was revealing my childhood to her so that she could have a better understanding of why I am the way I am.

It helped, but I'm still on probation with her and

rightly so.

I know I can never burden her with what happened that night with my mother's demise. It is too dark, too sordid, and I'm too scared of what her reaction will be.

Only Simon shares this horror with me, and we never talk about it.

Ever.

I have to live with what I've done, and that's it. Sometimes I revisit my youth, how this whole story began, but I cannot change it, only create a new story … my life restarted. And it's time.

Now I'm counting, and it's one year seven months and fifteen days since I've last abused alcohol.

And I will keep counting until the end of my life, because that's how long it takes to beat it.

The unpredictability of my status forced us to reassess, and, in the end, we decided not to have any children.

We couldn't take the chance. It was a hard decision, but the right one.

Shakira and I weren't willing to play Russian Roulette with the hand of fate.

Losing, meant our child or children losing and that would be unforgivable.

So, we learned to become enough for one another, as well as a promise to always revisit what got us to this place.

Help.

From our resource centre to the wider community. We weren't afraid to reach out. We became our own best advocates in order to stay well.

The great outdoors helped tremendously as well, and right now my new business is booming. We obtained commercial fishing rights in the Lake Windermere, which is a rare and precious commodity and now I spend my days doing what I love most. Fishing. But now with paying company. I couldn't be happier.

*

Sometimes I miss aspects of my former career in the banking world. The sheer genius of it, the money scrunching, the big victories, but I don't miss the cutthroat insincerity of it. I'm happy to leave that far behind and protect my mental health.

*

Shakira is happy too. She still models, still continues to enjoy what she does, but now that she's experienced the slowing down of everyday life here, she's far pickier about what she decides to do.

She continues also on her journey to process the events that first led her on this journey. The loss of her first husband. And I know with patience, love, and reflection, the grip of anger, anxiety, and fear will eventually subside.

She is, after all, an amazing woman.

So, there you go. This is my tale. How I succumbed, thrived, and hopefully survived alcoholism, and abuse, and the horrors of what my actions reaped on me.

But now I have Shakira back, and better coping mechanisms. I have the tools to force ahead.

So, at this point, I am happy, fulfilled but still incredibly complex.

I'm still a puzzle I have yet to unwind. My emotions are still fairly held in check, but I'm loosening. Unlearning forced responses. I'm getting there.

I have my friends, my love, and now a new business.

I have enough.

Shakira

Forgiveness is a big ask.

I've done so with Joe and now I'm ready to do it with the other person who played a big part in my life.

I'm at the cemetery. Apart from that day I put him down in this earth, I've never revisited.

I was far too angry, too disappointed, too sad.

And yet I am here now. And I'm still not quite sure how I feel.

Probably accepting, I conclude.

I unwrap my bouquet of flowers and kneel down at his gravestone.

"Hi David," I start. "I'm sorry I haven't come to see you before now. I know you've been waiting. But I wasn't ready. I think I'm ready now.

"I'm sorry, for abandoning you, just the way I accused you of doing.

"I know now that your action wasn't a conscious thought, unlike mine.

"I know that you loved me, and wanted the best for me, and that included standing up and saying no that day.

"You didn't know it would end like this, you were just protecting me, trying to scare him away. I think I can accept that now.

"So thank you for saving my life. If I had returned to that car, I would have been hysterical, and I would have been killed too.

"I know you knew this.

"I miss you; I will always love you, and I will always treasure our short time together.

"I want to tell you that I fell down but managed to get back up.

"Thank you for sending Joe.

"Thank you for sending him to breathe some life back into my empty lungs.

"He is kind, sensitive, loving, and fallible.

"There are many sides to him, some he doesn't even realise I know, but he would never hurt me. I know that.

"We fit.

"I want you to know that I'm going to be okay, that he'll look after me and that it is possible to love more than one person, and still be true in your heart.

"And I do love him. He makes me laugh, and sometimes cry, but always it fills me with tremendous hope.

"I trust him with my soul.

"So, go to sleep now, sweetheart, I'm sending you off to rest. I promise you I'm okay now. Go and find your peace, I've found mine and one day we'll cross paths again and I can say hello. That would be nice."

I get up and dust the dirt off my trousers. When I look around, to my surprise, I see Joe standing there. Looking at me with an expression I cannot discern.

"You okay?" he asks softly.

I wipe the tears from my cheeks.

"I'm going to be," I say in return. "How come you're here? How did you know ..."

He shrugs, looking slightly boyish when he does so.

"I just knew."

I nod, sometimes it's better not to prod, just to accept.

"Are you ready to come home?" He looks a little uncertain.

I walk up to him and lace my fingers through his.

"I'm home already."

Letters to Shakira

I did what I promised you. I went and got help.

But it's hard in here. It's a shit hole, and I don't know how long I will be staying.

I did what you asked though. Only saying.

*

I paid forty thousand pounds to be here, and I'm locked up like a damn child at 9 p.m.

They do some bullshit group therapy here and the nurse that is assigned to me is a fucking witch.

She rejoices in my discomfort, I swear. I'm in so much pain, she just tells me to take a fucking tablet, like that's going to make a difference.

I'm only sticking this out just to piss her off

And because I promised you too, of course.

*

Nurse Ratchet actually smiled at me today.

I agreed to come to the group therapy, and she cracked a smile!

Still bullshit, but I stayed to the end.

Thought a lot about you today.

*

I wrote to Tim Robbins today, the guy in my bank who helped oust me.

I told him I was sorry, that I understood why he had to let me go.

Feeling ashamed. Reflecting a lot.

I wish I could talk to you face to face; I wish I could have had just two more minutes with you that day.

*

Managed to get through today without feeling angry.

Hitting the gym hard.

It helps. A lot.

Looked in the mirror and decided I have to fix up.

Have a little ponch. Not big — but it's there.

Want to get rid, want to look good in case I see you again.

*

A man in here overdosed today. Died. I cried like a baby.

So scared. I want to see you again. Badly.

*

Good day today, got through without any pain meds. I can do this; I know I can.

*

Thinking about you again. Dreamed about you last night. You were with another guy. I shouted out to you, but you ignored me.

Can't blame you. Why would you want me?

I'm a mess. You're fucking beautiful, you can have anyone you want, why would you look at me? Probably don't even remember me.

*

The nurse and I had a nice chat today. I puked up, humiliated myself.

She made out like it was nothing. She didn't make me feel bad.

*

Went for a walk outside the centre. Went to the lake that is situated in the far field. Feel peaceful. Saw a couple of rabbits making out. Laughed hard for the very first time in a long time.

Wished you had been here.

*

Why didn't I talk to you that day when you asked me? If I could go back now, I would.

I would let you see what was inside of me, and maybe it wouldn't have got so bad.

I keep coming back to that.

And now I can't bear that I might not get another chance.

I need one more chance.

*

I hope you're happy, Shakira, hope that you get what you wish for, I miss your smile, the sound of your laughter. I see you so clearly.

*

Doctor said I'm making good progress, that I can go home on Tuesday.

Not sure I'm ready, I feel secure here. The only good thing is, maybe I'll get to see you.

I'll wait to adjust a little to the outside world again and then I'm coming to see you.

I hope you're still free.

If not, it'll be nice to say thank you anyway.

I couldn't have done this without you.

And I'm determined to succeed. I won't be a stain on anyone else again.

I'm going to succeed.

*

I messed up. I realise that now. I was so afraid that she would come after you.

Now I've put myself in a situation where I can be taken from you.

I don't want you to have to go through that again.

I'm so sorry.

I couldn't tell you. I couldn't bear to see the disappoint and yes, fear that will be in your eyes.

I didn't want you to think I'm a monster, that I could ever hurt you, because I couldn't.

I would rather die than do that. I would rather die.

I could feel myself spiralling out of control, I didn't understand what I did would come back on me like that. I thought I could handle it.

But I couldn't.

I know you saw that wine bottle I had hid away.

I felt like a piece of shit when I saw you cry.

And I understand why you felt you had to go.

And if I have lost you completely, then I deserve to.

Because I want you to be happy.

Every day.

But I also want you to know I'm not giving you up without a fight.

I love you so much, I'm going to keep trying. I'm going to do everything to put this right.

I'm going to win your trust again.

I'm prepared for all of this to go wrong, prepared to face the consequences.

But know this …

No one can love you like I do. Even if the worst does happen,

I will still love you the same for ever as I do now.

Nothing could change that. I will go through rehab, jail, storms – whatever. But I need to get back to you.

You're the only thing in my life that I really care about.

And I will never give up fighting for that.

Never.

*

Thank you, my wife, for loving me, and for giving me our son and our daughter.

We didn't plan to have them, but I know they are truly a gift from god.

They are the game changer.

If I didn't know before if I would make it,

I sure as hell do now.

From the moment I held them in my arms, I knew I would become a better man.

It's imperative I don't mess up, and I give my solemn vow here and now, that I won't.

I absolutely adore them, as I do you.

Do you know what it is to be loved unconditionally?

Do you know how tall I feel?

On top of the world, ten feet tall.

Family is everything to me

You, the kids, your mum and dad.

I'm surrounded by love.

I still find it easier to put this on paper then to actually tell you. But I'm getting better, all the time.

So here it is. My bundle of notes. Notes that I scribbled to you when I couldn't speak them out loud. Notes I wrote when I feared that I would never see you again.

Notes I felt I had to hide from you

What is terribly obvious is right from the beginning, you knew.

And you loved throughout, regardless.

I'm crazily in love with you.

And I will remain so, my love, for the rest of our lives.

Your Joey

ABOUT THE AUTHOR

I love writing. Always have, always will. I'm not perfect, but I write my perfect storm and hope you enjoy it. I dream of doing this for a living someday, but until then I continue to help patients and work and dream big.

Take Down and *Already Taken* by Allison Forbes are also available on Amazon in paperback and Kindle edition.